A LIFE WORTH THE
FLEETING SUNS

LEON HUET

Page 125, a translation of *Oy Tam Na Gori*, a Ukrainian folk song.

www.leonhuet.net

ISBN 1537291084
ISBN-13 978-1537291086

Cover Photograph: FreeImages.com/Chris Panteli

for Kitty

In January 2016, DARPA released information on a $60m Neural Engineering System Design program with the aim of developing an implantable neural interface able to provide data-transfer between the brain and electronics.

A few decades later …

'I am become Death, the destroyer of worlds.'

The Bhagavad Gita *(XI,32)*

Recollected by J. Robert Oppenheimer, one of the fathers of
the atomic bomb, following the first test detonation.

CHAPTER ONE

In appearance they were not very remarkable, though that was to underestimate them entirely. For Lior could sense something was wrong as soon as the plane turned to taxi towards the London terminal. The number of vehicles perhaps, or the tone of the pilot's voice.

Despite that, drifting forwards in the cold night air with a current of people towards the glow of the terminal building, he took Delphi's pale hand with his own. He was in his late-twenties, she a few years older, and he was not yet willing to let her go.

Two policemen in fluorescent yellow jackets emerged. Both gestured for Lior and Delphi to step out of the line of passengers. They looked around, but it was clear they were being asked to go quietly. Lior had used the opportunity to count the unmarked vehicles around him.

One of the police officers said that they matched the description of two individuals they had been asked to look out for and were checking passports.

When the last few passengers had passed by, Delphi lowered her voice and said, 'You've made a mistake. I'm an MI6 intelligence officer.' She produced her ID. 'This is an informant and we've returned from Russia with time sensitive information. You'll find that everything is in order.'

'I'm sure we will, ma'am,' the police officer said. A UK Border Agency officer came up behind him and he passed her the two passports. 'I'm only following orders. If you could just spare a few minutes of your time you'll soon be on your way.'

Delphi looked vaguely unimpressed, but Lior knew that such a reaction was understating things substantially. In the glass of the terminal building he could see that a convoy of police cars was slowly approaching from behind, snaking between two aircraft. And then, as airport stewards closed the double-doors into the terminal behind the last passenger, the world around them erupted into a cacophony of noise, flashing lights, sudden movements, thundering boots and the metallic linearity of semi-automatic carbines.

The two police officers in yellow jackets faded away into a mass of black-clothed armed police officers drawing closer from the unmarked vans. With the additional police and Delphi beside him he dared not risk anything now.

'Get on the floor. Get down. Get down. Get on the floor. Get on the goddamn floor.'

Lior and Delphi dropped to their knees. But an officer was at Delphi's arm helping her back to her feet.

'Not you, ma'am,' the wiry man said, and with some force he pressed her backwards into the arms of two men in suits.

'What are you doing?' she shouted. 'He hasn't done anything wrong, don't hurt him. He wants to help us.'

Lior had started to get to his feet as Delphi was taken away, but he was instantly kicked in the spine and had his arms taken behind his back by a tangle of hands. They pushed his now handcuffed wrists up between his shoulder blades. He submitted as a boot pressed his head against the tarmac. A muzzle stared down at his temple from a few inches away. They bound his feet then gagged him. Finally, he was lifted by his arms and legs onto a stretcher and strapped to it face down.

They evidently knew far more about him than he had anticipated. But besides the physical discomfort and feeling of dread, he felt a strange sense of liberation. He had been recognised for what he now was.

A blacked-out car had pulled up beside Delphi, the two men in suits still holding her. A door opened and a man leant out. His sharp jaw was set hard, heavy lips pulled tight. Black hair stood up in a short afro over his ebony scalp.

'Get in Delphi, you'll be able to see him back at the Circus.'

Delphi looked away, between the two men who were now shepherding her towards the door. Lior was being loaded into the back of a black Jankel armoured police truck. She eventually tore her eyes from him.

'How did you know we'd be on that flight?'

'I knew you wouldn't have shared everything with me, so I've kept records on every alias you've had since the beginning. Plus your op sec and pattern setting is really starting to slip.'

Delphi was taken aback for a moment. 'But you didn't know I'd return with him, Jared. You left me there, and I found him. I did my job.'

'Your job is to follow your orders. He's alive. He's here. But it's meaningless now. No one cares about Vosinsk anymore. He's second-page news when the world is on the brink of war.'

Delphi eventually got into the car and it pulled away.

'That may be true,' she said, looking out into the night. 'However, it may also be true that he is our last chance to stop it'.

Jared looked at her. She did not return his gaze.

'You should see what he has become.'

CHAPTER TWO

Deep below the basements of MI6 Building, in a cavernous bunker designed and built at the very end of the Cold War, the Chief of the Secret Intelligence Service, the Head of Cyber Division and two of its principal operations officers left the lift and walked for just over a minute through corridors and blast doors until they came to the security section. Around them other employees were busying themselves with computers, furniture and stores, getting the place ready for habitation.

Passing through security, Delphi and Jared followed the chief, C, into a room with a red lamp above the door. Edward, the Head of Cyber, was the last to enter. Delphi found herself in a dark recording and observation room. Along one side was a one-way mirror through which she could look into a brilliantly lit and sparse interrogation cell. There, at a metal table with wrists cuffed behind his back and feet chained to the floor, sat Lior.

He stared back at the glass as if he was looking directly at her. Delphi pursed her lips but otherwise didn't let any emotion show on her face. Though inside she felt utter devastation for letting Lior down so completely, and fear that he probably thought she had betrayed him.

'He really is quite something, isn't he?' C's long, regal face turned to Delphi. 'The team have run a quick scan already. Remarkable that all his synthetic elements grew in the space of two weeks. And you wouldn't know it to look at him.'

She nodded, not taking her eyes from Lior.

'And is this the extent of it? Rebuilt sections of his bone and muscle?'

'Well, the code entered his nervous system,' Delphi said. 'But in terms of what is visible, it looks to be anywhere that was injured when he fled from Vosinsk. What must be nanites in his body repaired the areas cybernetically.'

'And where did the nanomachines come from, I wonder?' C said, raising an eyebrow at Delphi. 'They can't have just materialised in his bloodstream because some kind of intelligence gained entry to his wetchip, to his brain.'

'The quartermasters will be able to tell us given time', Edward said. He was an angular, tense man with quick, green eyes and golden skin.

Delphi doubted that was true, and she was not one to bite her tongue. 'I imagine directed electromagnetic stimulation from his wetware by this intelligence gradually formed the first few, perhaps simple self-replicating synthetic compounds from the metals in his blood, and those created improved nanites, and so on, until he became who he is.'

'You certainly have your ideas then,' C responded.

'That she does,' echoed Jared.

Delphi glared at him. 'I don't know that it's right, I just read about this sort of thing growing up all the time. But now it's become reality.'

'A reality you have grown fond of?'

She thought for a moment about how to answer him, then said, 'He is a unique individual.'

'Indeed he is. Has anyone spoken to him?' asked C.

'Not yet,' Edward responded. 'We were waiting for you.'

'Good. Let's see what sort of reception we get.'

They left the room and a guard unlocked and opened the three-inch thick door to the interrogation room. Lior didn't turn to look at any of them. Didn't move at all.

C strode around to the front of the table and inspected Lior closely. Delphi stood by the door, guilt creating a pit in her stomach.

Eventually, C spoke. 'I am the Chief of the Secret Intelligence Service, MI6, and I wanted to speak to you personally now as we have so little time. You must understand that your actions did not set the world down the path to war. It was an inevitability. A consequence of our civilisation over-heating as it were, competing like a bag of snakes, as they so often have done in the past, so it comes to bear for us as well.

'Unfortunately, our civilisation now spans the globe and we have devices capable of destroying our way of life irrevocably for many years to come. As someone who shares responsibility for the security of the United Kingdom, I am left with no choice but to have you incarcerated in one of the deepest nuclear bunkers in the country, so that you may aid us in weathering the approaching storm as best we can, and crucially, in rebuilding a strong Britain, a strong Europe and a strong West generally once the remnants of us re-emerge into a brave new world.

'You will likely be able to withstand the fallout much sooner than a normal individual anyway, and the technology now within your person will undoubtedly help ensure we in the West are sufficiently advanced to run the new world order. Leading the vestiges of humanity towards a brighter future. And you will be our guide. What do you say?'

Lior didn't speak for a few moments, but then he turned his head to look directly at C as he replied. 'It is not too late to stop a war. Make an announcement. Parade me on the news. Inform Russia, China, the Arab states. Everyone you consider enemies. Why gamble with our planet, with billions of lives? The truth is you don't want to avoid it. A chance to start over, to rebuild the world, that's what you want, isn't it?'

'You certainly have an active imagination. I'll give you that.'

Lior stared back at him.

'The truth is the US, France and the UK are moving to pre-emptively strike tonight, whilst crisis talks are on-going and before clear Russian and Chinese aggression takes away any capability advantage we might hold. Before they also have the chance to attempt to neutralise our weapons systems through a cyber-attack dwarfing Vosinsk I might add. Even as I speak, an attack by the Chinese navy on a US destroyer that navigated through the South China Sea a few hours ago, in spite of outrageous threats from Beijing, has precipitated out-and-out conflict between the world's two superpowers.

'Since then, a number of satellites have gone offline and sleeper-agents are likely behind a number of reported sabotage attacks on infrastructure. The US hasn't got an appetite for that kind of war. Nuclear strikes, on the other hand, have a proven record of stopping protracted and costly conventional campaigns dead. The cogs are in motion. No one will stop them now. The decision has been made by people above my pay-grade, and it's only a matter of time.'

Having ignored her throughout the entire proceedings so far, Lior turned to look at Delphi. She was as incensed as Lior appeared at C's last statement, but she stayed silent and C continued. 'Let us not forget that the Russians have effectively declared war on *us*, nor of course that the Chinese have attacked the United States, the crux of NATO, for travelling through international waters.' C circled around Lior.

'You will not be believed in any case, and if you are, no one will care now. In fact, parading you in our hands as some kind of blessing, even without a demonstration of your components, could cause the Russians to act unpredictably.

'They could see the media distraction as an opportunity to strike – it's worked for them before. It could result in our destruction and them coming out relatively unscathed. In essence, showing you off to the world could hasten war, not stop it. People will watch you, enthralled for a few days. But will it stop all of this? Unfortunately, no. In any case, whether you are willing in this matter or not is irrelevant. You are not going anywhere. But you have nothing to fear; I'm sure any tests we carry out will be quite painless.'

'There is one thing,' Delphi said finally. 'The code seems to be designed to infect a system and then jump to another, but in doing so leave the original system irrevocably corrupted. If the code gets out of Lior, if a device is plugged into his wetware port, or by another means, then it'll likely result in his brain being permanently damaged. It's difficult to know exactly but every system that has had the code on it is useless now, corrupt. And that means Lior would be useless to us – you can't understand a system if it doesn't work.'

'Thank you, Delphi, I'm sure you have a great interest in Lior being kept alive, but I'm also sure that the best minds we have will be able to figure it all out once they've had a look at him.'

'Listen to her,' Lior snapped at C.

'They mustn't connect anything to him,' Delphi said. But finding no sympathy from C, she turned to Edward. She could feel anger rising in her chest. 'If anyone connects a device to his wetchip port it will kill him.'

And she added coldly, her voice low, 'And I will find whoever did it, so help me God.'

Edward stepped forwards, suddenly enraged.

'Delphi, outside now.'

Delphi looked at Lior, and he at her.

'I didn't tell them we were coming, it was Jared, he tracked my aliases and saw I was on that flight. I would never have left Russia if I'd known.'

Jared took Delphi's arm and pulled her to the exit. Delphi jerked out of his grip.

'I'm sorry, Lior.'

But Lior didn't look at her. Guards burst through the door and pulled her from the room as she shouted again. His eyes stayed fixed ahead.

CHAPTER THREE

Lior was left alone with the knowledge that someone would soon be along to question him. He didn't want to think about Delphi. He found it hard to believe she wouldn't have known, or hadn't anticipated this. Unless she had been blinded by recent events. So he sat and waited, burning with anger that a war would soon engulf the world. A war that he had helped cause. His ankles and wrists were chained, but his mind was still free to question whether he had, as Delphi had once told him, been driven solely by self-interest after all. Interest in extending what little time he had been allotted.

Aptly, an old fashioned cream clock hanging on the wall above the door caught his eye. He watched the second hand count down each minute like each one would be the last. Though he also found its rhythmic ticking soothing. In fact, he found his mind becoming still, the beta frequency waves decreasing. He continued to watch the second hand as a calm sense of control descended over him. But a recollection arose within his mind of what tonight might bring, and in response came a desire for time to stop, for this moment to be suspended, a snapshot of life on this planet to exist as it is now, before facing ruin and death.

And then, as he continued to follow the steady movement of the hand about its face, he began to notice what had at first been imperceptible: the gap between the ticks seemed to be dilating.

It was unquestionable. But he felt no different. Each tick became slower and slower. He held his gaze steady on the quivering hand, following its arc towards the vertical, willing it to still.

Then, after a few more drawn out seconds, its motion was arrested completely. It simply paused mid-tick, hovering over the number two. And yet Lior could think as he had before. His mind was free to contemplate – unshackled seemingly – by time.

He felt euphoric and wallowed in the endless moment, letting it sink into his being. The ramifications were too great to comprehend at once.

The position of the second hand still hadn't altered.

He tried to cast his eyes downwards, and simultaneously began to lift his hands to study them. But he couldn't move.

Then he noticed that in fact there was the slightest change to his field of vision, and he waited as it drifted downwards for what seemed like an eternity. When it met the floor his hands came into view, as if moving through water. The second hand had also moved slightly, now just after the number two. Time hadn't stopped after all, merely ground to a crawl. And yet his mind was as quick as ever.

He had felt fibres growing within his spine and up his neck, and perhaps they extended upwards, undetected because of the absence of sensory neurons in the brain. If they were metallic then the propagation speed of nerve impulses would have multiplied colossally. If the nanites within him had built superconducting lithium-lined graphene along his central nervous system and brain, then the wave propagation speed of electrical signals could effectively be the velocity of light.

He reasoned that if biological nerve impulses travelled at

a dismal two hundred and fifty miles per hour, and the wave propagation speed of lithium-lined graphene was approximately six hundred and seventy million miles per hour, then his brain was now perhaps two and a half million times faster than before. Or to put it another way, one second to others could stretch out for an entire month to Lior. So judging by the clock maybe he didn't have superconducting synthetic nerve fibres after all; or perhaps he hadn't yet harnessed his full potential. Either way, the rest of his body was as sluggish as ever, his muscles limited by the stimulus of motor nerves. Unless, he reasoned …

At that moment a hatch at the top of the door edged open by an infinitesimal fraction, and the movement immediately brought Lior back to an organic passage of time, interrupting his thoughts. It felt as though he had returned from another reality.

A guard opened a viewing hatch, glanced around the cell, then swung open the door.

Two armed guards entered followed by a late middle-aged man in a charcoal suit. He placed a tablet on the table and then sat down opposite Lior without looking up. He clasped his hands together and thought for a moment as one of the guards locked the door.

Whilst he waited for the man to speak, Lior decided that he would slow the passage of time, kick his chained ankles against the reinforced table leg, dislocate his shoulders and avoid any lumbering strikes from the two guards whilst knifing them in the back of their necks with the sides of his hands. Every armed officer in the building could try to prevent him escaping, but he had the growing sense that no one could stop him now.

Despite this, he was only just beginning to understand the

changes that had occurred within him, and only just beginning to understand how to control them. And he didn't know exactly what he could do to stop a nuclear holocaust, but he knew that he was linked to it, and he was compelled to do everything he could to stop it. He would not stay underground like a rat, weathering a storm that killed billions, ravaging the world with fire then years of darkness.

Then the man opposite him spoke. 'I've worked with Delphi for a number of years, and she's never acted quite like she has over you. You seem to have caused a bit of a stir generally, to put it mildly. I'd like to go through the last couple of weeks with you. To make sure we've understood things correctly and to avoid any wrong assumptions. So why don't we start with when you met?'

The lights in the interrogation room flickered off for a second, plunging it into darkness. When they came back on two seconds later the guards were slumped on their sides and Lior was holding the set of keys.

However, the question's echo, still just about audible to Lior, made him recollect with absolute clarity when he had first set eyes on Delphi. And in his mind the previous two weeks were replayed from that moment in a fraction of a second. He had been in a bar. It had been just another day.

Then she had walked in looking to take away everything he had worked for. Though he hadn't known it at the time.

He hadn't known a lot of things about her.

Or about himself.

CHAPTER FOUR

Delphi sat down at the table, looked up at Lior and smiled a knowing smile that made him feel as though he was being seen unclothed. 'What's the stud in the side of your head?' she asked after a few moments, reaching up and holding it lightly between the pad of her thumb and forefinger, her ivory skin brushing his temple and dishevelled hair.

'A wetware port,' Lior said, his dark eyes on hers.

They were sitting at a table only a row back from the front of the bar. Outside, cars and pedestrians meandered along the narrow London street, the earthy smell of rain blowing in and mixing with the oak and a Miles Davis record.

'I've never met anybody with one before. I've seen them, though – in an article.' Delphi smiled again. 'So it works?'

'Our minds don't care where a signal comes from,' he replied, his Eastern European lilt rising and falling. 'They just learn to interpret it, yes? Whether it's from a sensory nerve or a cochlear implant, it's just information.'

Delphi leant forwards, her fingers supporting her angular chin, and a sense of self-belief rose within him. He paused in case she wanted to change the subject, and adjusted his black-framed glasses – pushing the bridge back with a forefinger – but she just watched him.

'Our minds learn to use any information they receive, just as replacement limbs use the information sent by the mind,' he went on. 'Light becomes vision, pressure becomes touch.

And for me, when I pay it attention, the stock market feels like the open sea. I know what moves it, and I know instantly.'

He swirled his wine into an eddy then swallowed a mouthful and replaced the glass. 'But really, it's like trying to describe sight to someone who's never; they're metaphors, though the sensations are as real to me as the music playing now.'

He leant back as she studied him, dimples forming in her cheeks as her face rose to complete a smile her eyes had already begun. 'And what do you know about me?' she asked.

'Enough.' He smiled back.

She averted her eyes and swept a finger around the rim of her glass. He used the time to look at her closely, at the rips in her tight jeans, crossed so that one of her suede ankle boots hung out from beneath the table, inches from his calf.

Eventually she said, 'Wouldn't it be tempting to … communicate with each other like that? Wordlessly. Think of the things we could share.'

She let the thought sit there between them, hanging in the air like a feather. Then she gazed out of the window over Soho's cobbled streets, at distant figures blurred by the rain.

'What if I died, what would you know in those last moments that I wouldn't live to tell you?'

He broke the silence with a whisper. 'Have you heard of Atma?'

'Perhaps.'

'Where?'

'A little bird.' Her voice was smoky with the wine.

'Perhaps you should be introduced.'

'If I am, is there any going back?'

He leant away in his chair. 'Maybe.'

'Are you going to come back?'

'When it's time I don't intend to.'

She cocked her head at an angle so that her hair was bunched in one hand. 'Wouldn't you miss me?'

'You could come too.'

'I'm not sure it'd be the same,' she said, then looked down and danced her fingers over the grain of the table.

'Besides, I don't know that I want to live forever.'

Lior walked with Delphi to the end of the street in the rain where they parted with lingering glances. Then he took the tube back to Bow, east London, and walked to his tower block and took a lift to the fourteenth floor. Crossing over to his apartment, his front door unbolted just before he pushed it open and it closed behind him with a click. The lights came on around him, though he looked at the lamp on his desk to make it a little brighter. His computer's screen came to life and Nick Cave's *No More Shall We Part* started playing throughout the apartment at his request. He glanced over at the windows framing the London skyline and the blinds began to roll down to give him some privacy as he got to work.

Sitting in his desk chair he poured a shaky finger of vodka and knocked it back in one. The hum of his computer linking up with a string of randomly selected IP addresses from around the world as he accessed darknets did little to comfort him. He longed to get started, to work towards alleviating his fear of dying and quiet his disruptive mind. But he knew the importance of his computer's set-up process: it covered his tracks.

When it was complete, he wrote a message:

Bury this file and I'll find out how deep you can go.

Embedding a code he had created specifically to test another he sent the message to Delphi with a single thought. She had been surprisingly well turned out for a crooked banking analyst. Probably resentful of her boss's salary and benefits. Or bored. She seemed the type – spoilt, and uninterested with it all. Still, however she got her kicks her work spoke volumes. And there was no denying how alluring she was, despite the air of arrogance.

If she passed his test she would help expand Atma's network. Just as he was doing now. The enabling of a better world: a virtual afterlife for all those able to upload before they draw their last breath. An extension to the time we are otherwise allotted.

He started at the top of the tasks given to him and connected to an encrypted URL. The screen that opened was in Russian and Lior mouthed the commands and warnings fluently before starting his password identification software. Within a minute a match was made and he was an administrative user in a distant computer server. He mouthed the file names saved on a server in front of him, following a centralised file plan into the depths of a complex folder structure, intent on burying his program deep within it.

The names on the screen didn't mean anything to him unfortunately – he had hoped to find a top-secret relic from the Soviet period. So he just opened a folder at random and then, to check he had full read/write authorisation before leaving his poisoned gift, opened a file called 00-594-37-61V-140603- 20010503. He yawned whilst it loaded and let his eyes settle on a stack of printed paper beside the display.

He picked it up and read the first page absentmindedly, flicking a pencil between his fingers. 'At a point or passage of time in the twenty-first century – which could already be occurring – humankind will collectively face a choice. Either we'll manage to avoid destroying civilisation, by brokering a permanent form of sustainable international stability and cooperation, based on achieving technology that will make problems of resource scarcity and competition obsolete: i.e. a singularity that we cannot possibly see beyond as the rate of innovation will be exponential; or we'll manufacture an extinction level event, which, if we survive, will take us back to the dawn of man. This would at least solve the problem of why the skies are so quiet: intelligence inevitably destroys itself …'

Something caught his eye and Lior glanced up at the screen – the file he had opened had expanded into a window before appearing to start a process of uncompressing.

Strange, he thought, flinging the papers onto the desk.

Sub-folders appeared, and from these further folders, as if the file was opening into a larger program. The file size had already increased ten-fold; far more than most high-end compression applications are capable.

And then it stopped. And another window opened, and another. A seemingly random stream of digits racing through them, bursting into life. It was as if a pattern encrypted within the code had duplicated and split off, unfolding like a seedling opening and embracing life. The once minuscule blueprint was being replicated and building itself into a larger structure, the file size soaring exponentially.

And then it stopped again, and the screen cleared – the windows cascading in on themselves. Lior stared at them with bafflement that only increased when servers previously accessible from the login started going offline. Whatever it was, it seemed to be causing a large amount of damage in the Russian network. Time to leave.

But as Lior selected the log-off button at the bottom of the screen, a download to his personal computer started, denying him permission. 'What the hell?' he hissed.

He tried to kill the link from the command prompt but nothing happened. The download was twenty gigabytes and counting.

His only option now was to sever any connection to the hack as quickly as possible and then clean up after it. He looked at the power button on the side of the screen.

No, he thought, I can't leave this. What if there's no getting back in? So he watched as the download continued; half a terabyte was really stretching his set-up given current usage – he hadn't archived anything in weeks. Within seconds the system would crash.

Suddenly, the hacked Russian desktop went black and he lost access. It took a moment for his operating system to come back to life, and then the reality of what had just happened hit him – a window displaying '*Download Complete*' hung in the corner of his screen like a life sentence. In the space of a few seconds, something had just left a direct path between his own computer and a breached high-security Russian government server. He swore, eyes wide, his snappy intonation hitting the 't' like the crack of a bullet.

Lior's fingers found their way to his forehead, the pads of his thumb and forefinger circling the protrusion of the wetchip out of habit, as he whipped through possible responses to the black hole he was in.

This would end everything – the knot in his gut told him as much. His body knew things were about to implode. He was falling again and the terror of it suddenly hit him like the shock of impact. There was no option, he was going to have to attempt to get back in and delete all evidence. That is, if anything was left at the other end.

But then his computer opened a net link without him instructing it to. Or had he? One drawback of his mind-computer interface was that the line between a mere idea and actual conscious intention occasionally blurred. Sometimes it was difficult to know where the boundary between him and his machine lay.

He didn't have long to confirm either way, however, as his messaging accounts opened of their own accord and connections were made with his contact lists. The hacker had become the hacked.

'It's not possible.'

Just then the cloud link reached his internet service provider's networks, threatening to unleash itself on half of Europe. That was enough for Lior, and he disconnected from the net with a single thought. The computer activity stopped.

He twisted his silver ring around a trembling finger, thinking. This was bad. Really bad. It threatened everything. He suddenly longed to be a student again, to have nothing to contemplate but the very foundation of consciousness and matter.

Then a window opened on his display. The computer's wireless connection had found his phone and opened its access systems. He snatched it and stabbed the power button.

Whatever the hell this was, it was trying to get out and right now it was like an animal testing its cage. Sure enough, his wall-mounted display burst into life, a snowstorm whipping up on the screen, and then it flashed on and off like a strobe light while the speakers spewed out a garbled stream of distorted pulses.

'This can't be happening.'

And then the intelligence found an open door. The folder to his wetchip connection opened up on the screen, and Lior's face dropped.

'No.'

His hand shot to his head and simultaneously a stream of code poured into a display window. A silver whirlpool swirled inside the stub on his temple, a storm of data raging through it. He closed the folder in horror, a head rush building in intensity so that he could hardly stand. He reached for his wetchip to unscrew it, knocking the last of the vodka onto the floor, the smashing glass cutting through the quietness of the night. But it was too late. With the same suddenness that the code had started uploading, it stopped. A window popped open, '*Upload Complete*'.

There were a few moments of stillness as Lior's head rocked forward in a stupor, and then against the receding sound of the machine's fan, the computer screen corrupted and switched off. This plunged the room into darkness with a low whir that softened and became the static hum of deep night. Specks of red standby lights from the room's electrical equipment flickered out like boats sinking in a sea of black.

When Lior next looked up he was standing on another world, on a barren plane beneath unfamiliar stars.

CHAPTER FIVE

Our sun, colossal and blinding, cast a shrinking crescent over Earth, as it continued turning, engulfing the Eurasian continent in shadow. Winter gripped the north – a vast snowy tundra stretching across Russia, where in the west a forest encroached the shore of the Arctic Ocean. There, many miles from other settlements, a scientific outpost weathered the cold with little light escaping from the rectangular buildings and skeletal radar structures. It sat looking out over the White Sea, one dish angled at the heavens staring up like an unblinking eye.

Boris Krakow sat in front of a workstation in the dark empty control office of the listening outpost, a battered Russian Synodal Bible open in one hand, reading glasses on the tip of his ruby nose. His thin lips whispered as he read from John 3:16:

> *For God so loved the world that he gave his only begotten Son, that whoever believes in him shall not perish but have eternal life.*

He re-read the words silently. Trying at once to reinforce them in his mind, whilst subconsciously looking for any fault in the sublimeness of them as a true act of God. Outside it was pitch black, and he caught his reflection in the window, for a moment thinking there was a stranger looking in through the glass, a weathered old man who had miraculously made his way into the camp.

He had aged a great deal since the photograph he kept in his wallet of him and his son was taken, just two weeks before he died. The tufts of white hair, baggy eyes, and leathery skin a stark reminder of how old his son would have been – an adult now, maybe with children of his own.

The death in itself brought grief, but the pain of losing someone so young also delivered the hopeless acute agony of the life that was yet to be lived, but now never could. The casual tearing out of a page of history, which tore through Boris more poignantly with every passing year, with every added thought of what might have been. His aged features were nothing but a constant reminder of those years and of the eternal life he prayed his son now led. But his faith wavered, caught in the ebb and flow of his search for meaning in a universe of unfathomable waste and seeming emptiness.

He had waited more than fifty years for a confirmation, but if God spoke to him, it was not in the silence from the heavens he so avidly listened to.

However, as he placed the Bible on the desk, darkness suddenly descended around him, enveloping him, drawing space inwards until he existed only within the inch between his redundant eyes. He heard the heating and computer cooling fans turn off with a drowning whirr, and he drew breath, frozen to his chair in astonishment.

After a few seconds, batteries in the low-level lighting turned the all-pervading black to a blue ultraviolet glow. But the computers remained lifeless.

Boris sat staring at the screen in front of him in astonishment. Only faint strip lights running down the centre of the room towards the emergency exit illuminated what little there was around him – mostly empty chairs and rows upon rows of monitors and computer control panels. He was like a statue, only snow falling outside the long horizontal windows stretching around the large room betrayed that time had not simply stopped, each flake catching faint moonlight in its descent.

He took a deep, rasping breath and then sighed and looked around him. He was alone – no one was there to confirm what had happened. It was up to him to deal with it. He shook his head at the screen and hit the keyboard.

Nothing.

He stood up and made his way over to the light switch by the door of the office and tested it twice. Again, nothing. The entire complex was offline. The embedded batteries were keeping emergency strip lights on, but they would probably only last a few hours. In the dead of winter one of the last places on Earth you would want to be is northern Russia, and they weren't due a scheduled visit for a couple of weeks. Soon the temperature would drop and he'd be forced to leave the buildings and try to take refuge in the military unit across the compound, past the nearest row of trees.

He tried the landline phone but it wouldn't dial. Then he took out his cell phone. 'What on … ?' The screen was black and it wouldn't turn on. Moments before it had had almost full battery.

He sat back in his chair and looked around again. It was eerily quiet. What on Earth could have knocked out every computer system? Even cell phones? This wasn't right at all. Everywhere was dark and shadows played across the space around him.

He rose and padded along the row of computers, then out into the hallway and down the stairs. In the stairwell, he could hardly see the hands in front of his face.

Along the corridor on the ground floor, he found the electricity cupboard and opened the door. No hum of power, no tripped switches, no glowing screens.

But then Boris froze. Yegor and Vladimir. They were working at the other end of the complex on a pump in the old bunker. Where the supercomputer had been installed ten storeys down.

'My God', he whispered.

They could have only minutes to live.

He fumbled out of the room then marched out into a bracing dawn. The thermometer at the door read −20°C. His hands were frozen within seconds, his moustache grew frosted with moisture from his nose. But still he pushed forward through two or three feet of snow, across the open square between the two sets of buildings, leaving a haphazard trail of footsteps in his wake. Despite spending most of his time tracking satellites and stars, Boris could be a bull of a man when he needed to be.

He moved steadily. His legs were beginning to burn but he fed on the heat they generated. With each yank upward and stamp through the powder into the ice below, he kept his eyes on the bunker entrance.

Lior snapped back to reality in his chair and, gasping for air, stumbled out of the sliding doors onto a balcony illuminated by streetlights. He had had a vision of another realm, of some kind of wilderness stretching away into infinity around him. Above were stars that seemed too bright to be real. A blurred figure had been approaching him from the distance. The figure was calling something made inaudible by the wind. *Say?*

... *Stay? Stay clear?* He couldn't make it out and before the figure had reached him the vision fell away.

'What is happening to me?' he said, whilst fighting to regain control of his panicked breathing and trembling nervous system. Beneath him in the tower-block's shadowy car park a white sports-coupe came to life. Its full beam cut through the darkness, and wipers thrashed across the windscreen. Then the alarm sounded over the empty concrete, resounding down terraced streets, and the dashboard display switched on, a red alarm light flashing in its centre.

Lior's wetchip swirled a pearly-silver and he suddenly realised with panic that if he had become a vessel for a malign code trying now to unleash itself on another system, then he was just a few seconds from ending up like his computer, and the Russian network before it: dead.

Without wasting a heartbeat he ripped the wetchip from his head and let it drop to the floor between bloodied fingers. The car's windscreen wipers stopped, the lights turned off, the computer display went black and silence rang out like a siren, a static background hiss matching the grey fuzziness of the city.

Lior looked out over the lights of London before losing focus as if he was accelerating downwards through a vacuum. He lost balance, and stumbled back into the apartment, spinning into a leather armchair. His body jolted uncontrollably, his head thrown back in spasm. Then each breath became shallower and the thump in his neck's artery reduced until it was a trickle. With a terrifying speed, Lior found his awareness fading, all thoughts clouding over. He struggled to hold on. His concentration screaming against what he could only presume was death.

With all the authority he could summon, he commanded himself to stay awake, to cease the downward spiral into an unending void. His mind almost thrusting claws into sand running down the insides of the inescapable pit that was his fear.

But it was hopeless.

Perspiration created a glossy film across his skin and his vision darkened as unconsciousness took him.

With all his might, Boris smashed against the inert electronic door leading to the bunker lift. His shoulders were bruised and joints raw from the punishment. He was drenched in sweat, and red from exhaustion, white tufts of hair stuck to his forehead.

Ten storeys down, two thousand gallons of groundwater from the White Sea had seeped into the basement of the bunker, engulfing the pumps. Once the bunker had merely been susceptible to damp, but as the sea level rose with the melting ice sheets a few kilometres north, the water table breached the clay subsoil and hit sand. Work was almost complete on the installation of the supercomputer, and rather than abandon the project, computerised pumps were fitted that continuously protected the storey above from flooding. The trouble was the pumps needed servicing, as well as the supercomputer itself. Yegor and Vladimir – old friends who had spent most of their lives working at the naval shipyard in Severodvinsk – were employed because they could do both. But no one expected the computers to corrupt. Power maybe, there was a backup generator for that. But not computers. Not now. Not in the middle of the twenty-first century.

No pumps. No lift. No emergency stairs. With the

addition of the computer cabling and infrastructure, there just wasn't the space.

Boris tried jamming a length of piping between the edge of the outer door and the frame again, but it was hopeless. He stopped and strained to listen over his panting breath. He couldn't hear anything from behind the blast-proof doors; forty minutes without a working pump down there was too long for any hope to remain. And by the time he got to the military guardroom, it would be approaching an hour since everything had shut down. Not that he could think of any way they could help.

Only now would he accept there was nothing more he could do. Tears running freely down his cracked skin fell to puncture their own graves in the snow.

The beat of a rotor blade thrummed in the distance and a tiny flashing green dot appeared on the horizon. Boris dropped to his knees, knowing that others could save him from hypothermia in the open air, his exposed undershirt soaked to the skin. A breeze whisked ghostly pockets of clouds across the starry sky and he looked up, caught by their movement. But he looked straight beyond them, to the stars themselves. And further still, into the depths of space. At the heavens. But he found no comfort, no poignancy from the entirety of all existence.

And no trace of what he truly sought.

Divinity.

CHAPTER SIX

In the central office overlooking the Thames at 85 Albert Embankment, the Chief of MI6 sat across from the Head of Cyber, on low padded chairs in front of a large walnut desk. C's leathery olive skin and a long roman face held patient but firm eyes fixed on the man opposite him. He spoke. 'Edward, the people who destroyed your family are beyond our reach, and you must now get on with your life. Many of us make truly awful sacrifices in our line of work, and you top that list, but we do it regardless, so that others do not. I know that and you know that.'

Edward was watching blurred and sparkling lights from the city play over the river. His shoulders were hunched forwards and his fingers pressed together so that their pads had turned white.

He looked up, 'It's been a year. A whole year, C. And we've got nothing. It happened in broad daylight in the middle of the city, with all our resources at our disposal and poof – like a puff of smoke the people behind this are gone.' His voice was thin and clipped, and he held his eyes on C's, his face hard.

'I will get on with my life, sir, once those bastards are no longer getting on with theirs.'

C placed his drink on the glass table between them and leant forward. 'Now look here, Edward, I can't imagine what you've been through, I really can't. I've cashed large favours on this. I've personally flown to Moscow – as the head of the Secret Intelligence Service, and as your friend. I don't need to justify myself to you. I've done all I can. And this does not put it to bed; if leads arise we will follow them and refer them to the appropriate agencies as necessary. But, one year on, you must find yourself again, for you and for them. Retribution will not bring them back.'

'It won't, but the people who killed them must suffer a consequence, otherwise it's as if it means nothing. They died for nothing. I'm sorry, but I can't live with that. Nor should anyone.'

There was silence.

'You're not suggesting anything underhand, of course.'

'Underhand?' Edward said, smiling. 'I wouldn't want to undermine the overt nature of our organisation.'

C didn't smile back.

'I am not, sir,' Edward consoled him, his face dropping. 'I merely wish to let you know that, for me, it hasn't ended. Nor will it.'

'There's nothing else you need to tell me?'

'No, only that your scotch has got worse.' With that, he stood. 'I should go.'

'I'll be right behind you,' C said, checking tomorrow's appointments. 'Aisha's got tickets to Coriolanus at the Garrick.'

Edward pulled his mouth into a smile. It can be done, C seemed to be saying. One can start over.

Nevertheless, as he reached the door, C sat back and said, 'Edward. I hate them as much as you. The whole rotten lot. If you ask me, sometimes I think we should have met them on the plains of Ukraine years ago. Called bluff to their Maskirovka doctrine of deception. Put them back in their box de-masked and be done with it. But we didn't, and now we're having to deal with this whole thing about the Arctic dictated to us, not to mention the Middle East; and we live with that.'

Edward looked back at C, an ageing giant of a man whose frame reclined in the leather chair like a resting mantis. Arching over, a lone lamp cocooned him in a glow against the cold city lights visible through the floor-to-ceiling windows. Eventually, Edward said, 'Bold actions have created this world, I agree. But they can also destroy it. Goodnight, C.' And he slipped through the doorway into the labyrinth of MI6 Building.

That evening, Edward decided to cross the Thames before driving home. He wanted something from the night – the chilled air, a sense of the world around him. But beneath it all, he walked halfway across Vauxhall Bridge and looked down because the elements against his skin and the importance of all of life amounted to nothing. Everything just added to his pain.

The dark water churned below and he leant over so that he could see more clearly where he would hit it. It was a clean drop.

An emptiness tore at his insides, creating an unbearable desolation within him, and he looked up once more, perhaps for the last time at the city. Its illuminations reflected in his bleary eyes, whilst behind them he saw his lightly freckled wife and their two girls, smiling in matching lily-white dresses. All dappled with light untouched by branches heavy with apples. He could smell the jasmine Isobella had planted.

It was too much for one mind to endure and he leant forwards so that gravity would finally take him. But the pain stemming from what had happened, as he faced its conclusion, turned slowly. It became, as he clung to the only thing he could feel within him, a chain reaction in which a thought arose in his mind: Why should I suffer and not those who did this? And this thought directed his pain at them, and with the sense of injustice at the circumstances he found himself in, anger rose from within, clouding his entire being.

And then came hatred.

Adrenaline flooded his veins and he ripped paint off the steel handrail with his fingertips. The dark river slapped at the concrete feet of the bridge below.

He had been here before, sure, whether handling a knife, or on a balcony, or waiting for a train. But each time there was less in his way. The intention was purer. The trouble was, the longer he kept it bottled up, the greater his hatred built. He wanted to destroy something. And he couldn't do that if he was dead.

Back in his empty home in Hampstead Heath, Edward stood in his unlit kitchen looking out into the garden; its lawn extending into shadowy depths where birch trees dotted the fence line. Around him the house stood dark.

After dinner – spaghetti accompanied by Puccini's opera *Turandot* on full volume – he took a bath in the dark, lying in perfectly still water, the silence broken only by the occasional drip from a leaking tap.

Bored of the ceiling, and the recollection of a disastrous cricket match he'd captained in his last term at Eton, he let his head loll to one side, allowing his gaze to rest on the Edwardian mantelpiece. In the middle sat a wooden frame – one side contained a photo of Leah and Tilly climbing a cherry tree, whilst the other was a script that read: *Daddy, our best adventures are yet to come.* He became lost in their brazen smiles and glistening eyes until tears cooled his sallow cheeks and the bath went cold.

He was sitting on the edge of his marital bed in a dressing gown when his phone started ringing. He waited for a good ten seconds before deciding to answer it, stabbing out a cigarette on the bedside table. 'Yeah?'

'Sir, the individual behind Vosinsk is almost certainly somewhere on UK soil.'

Of all the one hundred and ninety-two countries in the world, he had to be in this one. And now he'd have to find out what had happened in Russia and provide answers on demand.

Not now, not tonight. Vehemence grew at a system he had sworn to uphold and protect, but had turned around and torn out his heart. And now he had only a dark cavity in its place; a wintry river flowing through a barren wasteland.

Above, a storm was gathering.

CHAPTER SEVEN

Two days later Lior awoke at dawn, though his spent body remained slumped over the side of the armchair and he couldn't get up, nor feel the pain from a split in the side of his head.

His black thin-framed glasses were crushed against his bicep, its narrow ridge pinned across the bridge of his nose. Shards of a broken glass were scattered beside him across the floorboards. He strained his peripheral vision trying to make out whether there was somebody in the murkiness around him, imagining for a moment that he'd been shot in the head. But he couldn't see anything other than his computer equipment bathed in the light from a desk lamp, nor hear anything but the sound of a distant aircraft. Everything else amid the scatterings of electronics seemed still and silent.

He had awoken from dreamlike memories of his mother, of when he had moved her from the state-run psychiatric hospital in Kiev to a private clinic in the Eastern Carpathian Mountains. Somewhere the money he had started making in London would buy her proper, clean and attentive care, and somewhere the authorities could not find her should they find him.

His eyes blinked again, startling him. His body felt alien, he couldn't connect that they were his eyelids and it was his view of the world before him. His thoughts were erratic: memories of national service burst through him – the sound of gunfire and then streaks of orange tracers arcing against an inky sky from behind a scattering of pines. He heard someone speaking, but it was Gabriel, and he was a student in the back of a lecture hall, listening to his theories on nanites and computing. His gravel voice barking Ukrainian at a screen at the front, a mass of sprawling code whipping across it.

Binary numbers slipped through Lior's head, integrating, dividing, multiplying, factoring; and then they stopped as if waiting for a command. His spine jerked, concentrating his mind, and a tuft of thick hair fell across one eye. His nerves spasmed again, dragging his face over the back of the chair, trembling its wooden feet against the floor. His hands shook, but his breathing remained constant, albeit faint.

All of a sudden he was in the room. His senses came alive together and he found that his head throbbed, his mouth was coarse and dry, and the daylight scorched his eyes. When he tried to stand, his stomach clenched in a vain attempt to feed his intestine, and his legs almost gave way with feebleness. In that moment he knew he had been unconscious for a great deal of time, and the realisation of how close he could have come to death shook him greatly.

He saw flashbacks of the code downloading onto his computer, it entering his head. A glass smashing in the night. He looked over to his corrupted computer on the floor beneath the table. He picked it up and tried to turn it on. Nothing.

Out on the balcony he spotted his discarded wetchip, partially stained with dried blood, and picked it up. In the car park below the white sports-coupe the code had tried jumping to had gone.

He knew now he couldn't risk re-inserting his wetchip, and with that realisation he understood he might not ever again be able to cross the sublime barrier between man and machine. He might forever remain trapped in his mortal flesh. The vision was over. The gates to Atma closed before him without fanfare, without a change to the world. A world quietly going about its business on the streets below. And yet the course of his life was changed for eternity. An eternity that no longer included him.

He remembered the vision of a plateau beneath an alien sky and a figure approaching him. *Stay clear*, the figure had called. Was it a warning? Was it the code? He felt lost, hollow, but as though he was sharing his mind with something else. He wanted it to get out of his head, but not if that meant death.

Who can I turn to now? he thought, but caught sight of his emancipated reflection in a mirror and stopped. The dark hole in his temple, surrounded as it was by a tarnished silver ring, stared back at his harrowed eyes, eyes that hardly seemed his own, like an animal confronting another of its kind. But the separation was even more severe – he'd not seen mercurial, grey irises like his own in any other man.

His glasses …

He wasn't wearing his glasses. Nor contacts. And yet he could see clearly.

More clearly than ought to be possible.

In the mirror's reflection he could see a news program on a screen in an apartment across the street. A female journalist was talking to the camera outside the imposing façade of the Kremlin in Moscow.

The journalist went to footage of a barren landscape, a blizzard raging across it, thick forests heavy with snow clinging to the ground against a gale. Lior turned, moving to the edge of his balcony to get a better look, and he could see that at the top of the footage, in the distance through a line of tall pines, stood a high, steel fence topped with rolls of barbed wire. A speck of red light shone through the fuzzy image, and a military truck passed beneath it, stopping outside a low breezeblock compound that sprawled away out of view. Soldiers wearing fur hats jumped out of the back and headed towards a door, a man in a long, dark coat amidst them. At the top of the footage a tag stated that it was a live video feed of Vosinsk, North West Russia.

A red bar that scrolled across the bottom of the screen read:

Devastating cyber-attack on Russian military installation – two dead – a number of groups still claiming responsibility – international authorities working around the clock. Russia on severe threat warning.

It was the research station he had hacked into. Evidently military. He had accessed supercomputers opening paths through the net that would allow Gabriel to create Atma. It was he who had screwed up, it was he who the trail led to, and right then he knew it was he who had found himself responsible for what was seen as a devastating cyber-terrorist attack on the Russian military. Two individuals had somehow died and knowing that filled him with shock and remorse. He felt that he might vomit.

People in the US, Japan, Pakistan, Israel and France had already been arrested and dragged from their beds – his Tor darknet access having bounced his IP address through several layers of encryption so that it appeared to have come from their locations.

Images of a Siberian work camp flashed up in his mind.

'No,' he said. 'This can't be happening.' His hands gripped his hair and he paced back and forth, eyes wild, body bent over in anguish. And then, slowly at first but with growing resolve, the pacing up and down began to clear his head of the tormenting fears.

He stopped at the mirrored display, and with his attention now focused, thought the situation through step by step. His mind seemed to be able to centre itself with more clarity than usual. He knew what he had to do.

He found his wetware port's flesh-like cover and stuck it over the empty hole. Then he cut his messy hair short, showered and shaved. He wore his Chelsea boots, dark tailored trousers and his zip-up jacket, stuffing his wallet, a multi-tool, two phones and a handful of passports into its inside pockets.

Then he looked out at the world, at the grey cityscape surrounding two poplar trees across the square. The sun was behind him, but visible in the shortest glimmer from a random reflection in a window. It had turned orange from the atmospheric dust on the horizon as if the other side of the Earth were in flames.

Lior, hands stuffed into his coat's pockets against the cold, walked across the city from east to west, through Stepney back streets before picking up the river, its brine cloudy beneath a drizzly wintry sky. He trudged unnoticed past suits and long coats that swept along the pavements like leaves caught in the wind. With his illness he turned inwards, minimising the projection of any engagement with the world.

He stopped at an ATM in Tavistock Square and tried every debit and credit card he had, but with increasing desperation he found each had been cancelled. When the final one disappeared into the machine without trace his face went white. They had found every online profile he had. All his funds gone.

He thought only of his mother and his chest heaved, drawing in the icy air so that his eyes stung with tears. He paid the clinic looking after her from one of the cancelled accounts. It was in a fictitious name to minimise anyone following his profile to the only person he needed to protect. The only person who needed his help. With no money left and his identity uncovered there was no way he'd be able to meet the next payment due in a few weeks' time, let alone the months that would follow.

For the first time in many years, since he had been a small boy, his eyes pricked with tears. He shouldn't have moved her. He should have left her where she was, but he couldn't even bear the thought of that. He was an idiot, a stupid, incompetent imbecile. He wanted to be somewhere he could call home, with her. Not in this strange city. Not with his future torn from him.

For Lior now also knew that he and his mother could no longer follow others down the path towards eternity, let alone light the way. He felt a pang of loneliness more sharply than that of being socially separate from those around him. Now the other door closed on him, that of being connected to the virtual. And he couldn't see that further doors remained. He was forever alone, perhaps one of the last of his generation to die.

But why? What could live inside him now? And who could have created it? He must have been framed, or used as a sacrificial lamb. But it was just a random file picked from thousands. Unless any of them would have triggered the virus, the code, whatever it was. The thing more destructive than any lines of programming he had ever seen, let alone created. But there was only one man who knew, indeed who told him to access the server. Gabriel. But why would Gabriel want to destroy the quantum computers so vital to his work? It didn't make sense.

In any case, he was the only man Lior knew who might be able to provide answers, and even reverse his fate. If the authorities caught him now he would probably never see Gabriel or his mother again. He would be locked away with a virus locked within his mind. Or worse, they would investigate, opening the gates for the virus to spawn, leaving him a lifeless and corrupted shell. He had to get answers and he had to recover the funds he had lost. He had to find him.

Lior pulled himself together and continued north, finding a state-backed payphone near Euston Station, still in existence in case of national emergencies. He gripped the receiver tightly and waited, counting the beeps. But finally Gabriel's phone answered for him. Lior listened for a few seconds, unsure of what to say. He didn't know what, if any, message would help, and didn't know how long he might have to wait for him to return the call. He hung up.

He could disappear, work cash in hand. Attempt to make contact. But what if the code in his wetware port started to affect him? What if he couldn't reach Gabriel? And what of his mother?

He was within a stone's throw from a means of transport to the continent. But glancing right, St Pancras International Station looked to be a fortress guarded by armed police ready to respond to a supposed terrorist threat with lethal force. He had only a few crisp notes in his wallet. Nothing like enough to board a maglev Eurotunnel train to the continent.

He looked to the sky momentarily, drinking in the saturated clouds. And then, taking a risk unlike any he had taken before, he entered more coins into the payphone and dialled.

CHAPTER EIGHT

Delphi walked through the entrance of the grand Victorian St Pancras International Station and surveyed the surroundings systematically, drawing her arms across her leather jacket to keep out the cold. In the distance, she could make out a lone figure standing in the shadow of a column across from the Embracing Couple, a towering bronze statue on a mezzanine floor.

The figure appeared to be poised with a perfectly straight back, but leaning slightly forwards as if ready to bolt. For someone who had lived his life blending seamlessly in the maze of the city he now, to the trained eye at least, jarred obviously with the scene around him. He didn't appear to be looking at any one thing in particular, just watching everywhere like a fly.

He looked more dishevelled than when they had first met: his hair as wild as his eyes despite it being shorter, and his creased, white shirt stuck out above and below his jacket.

Delphi couldn't see anyone hanging around with nothing else to do but keep an eye out, so he was more than likely alone. The rendezvous allowed him a lot of options should anything go wrong, though. Despite the containment of the station, there were enough staircases and exits to keep a team of operatives constantly fighting to stay one step ahead of a target's intention. Delphi scanned the hidden faces she could see dotted about her now.

Then she looked back at Lior. He was looking straight at her. The intensity was unnerving. He knows, she thought. But then why is he still here? She held her ribs tightly, and smiled as candidly as she could manage, her large mouth flashing a bright row of teeth as the clouds thinned and a pale ray of sunlight fell through the high windows. She bit her bottom lip awkwardly afterwards, an old habit from when she was younger and ashamed of a bucked incisor. I need to stop doing that, she told herself. Just relax.

Lior's face remained hard and unreadable. He nodded as she approached. 'Thanks for coming,' he said quietly. He smiled.

Delphi came to a stop six feet away.

'Well, I was intrigued.' She swept loose strands of hair behind an ear.

'How did I do?' Not too much, she thought, hold it back. See where he goes.

'Do you have any cash?' He looked up at her expectantly, ignoring her question; his dark, narrow eyebrows rising like scythes. His face was gaunt – it was going to be hard trying to convince him that she was actually interested. Thankfully he seemed to have lost any tact he might have possessed the night they met.

And yet his eyes were alive and gripped her attention.

She narrowed hers and shot back, 'You want to borrow money, is that it?'

'You heard about Vosinsk?'

She looked hard at him. 'Oh, you're going to need a lot more than just cash.'

He shifted awkwardly then looked up and said, 'I hacked it. But someone set me up, I didn't mean to cause any harm.'

'Half the damn world is looking for you.'

'Well, they're looking for the wrong guy.' He didn't take his eyes from her's.

'What happened then? Who should they be looking for?'

'I don't know. All I know is that for the first time in my life I need … help.' He fumbled with his hands. 'The virus … the virus jumped into my wetchip.'

'You're not serious.' Her eyes narrowed and she looked for the absent silvery stud in his temple. 'Why would you think that?'

'It happened in front of my eyes. I was just checking a random file in Vosinsk, I was working on …'

'Atma?'

'Yes, Atma,' he whispered, 'and then this code corrupted everything, and jumped to my computer, tried to get out anyway it could, it corrupted everything in my flat, it expanded so fast I couldn't control it, and then it found a door –'

This was the most she'd ever heard him say in one breath; he was visibly shaken. She knew he was telling the truth. But she played along interrupting, 'Come on, Lior, you're saying your wetware has been infected with a computer virus? What makes you think that is even possible?'

'It shouldn't be possible – of course, it shouldn't. The wetchips just receive digital data, encode them as sparse distributed representations and let the brain interpret the electrical impulses generated. And vice versa. But it happened, believe me.'

She pointed at his temple. 'Where is it now?'

'The code tried to jump out of me, so I had to rip it out. You know what happened at Vosinsk.' He glanced up then stepped back into the shadows, spooked by pigeons taking flight from a ledge above. He continued from the darkness, 'I need to find Gabriel.'

'How are you going to do that?'

'I need enough for a train to Kiev. Five hundred Euros. I'll pay you back online in a week.'

'Is that where he lives?'

He paused, then said, 'Maybe.'

She held his gaze then looked away, picked out a face in the crowd, caught herself and stared down at her feet. She didn't want to push him too hard for intelligence on Gabriel at such a delicate stage, especially given how panicked he was. It could blow everything.

'I could put the ticket on credit. Let me see your passport.' She stared at him, as he studied her, desperate and alone. Eventually, he reached into his inside pocket and produced one for a Lithuanian. Carl Sgie. Lior knew his identity wasn't linked to anything.

'Don't move,' she said, snatching it from his hands.

'Wait –' But she was striding across the hall and he sunk back into the shadows.

Delphi evaluated the situation: should she have Lior tried and found innocent of either creating or intentionally spreading the virus? Or should she take a chance on finding Gabriel, a man wanted by the security services of a dozen or so countries around the world, a man she had shaped a career around finding? As soon as she was out of earshot, Delphi called Edward, head of the Cyber Division. 'Who do we want, sir: the sheep' – she flexed her free hand then clenched it – 'or the shepherd?'

'If that's all you've got I'm passing this over to the Met Police,' he replied. 'They can bring him in.'

'But he said it himself without any reason to lie: he doesn't know who it was, he wants to find out. And he knows where to start looking. That's a huge amount more than we've got and he's got the cover.'

'You've got yours.'

'I was a single night in; Gabriel doesn't know me from Adam.' Silence. 'With your permission, I'll accompany him to the location.'

'You're out of your mind.'

'If we arrest him now we break his cover. I want to use it to our advantage.'

'Out of the question. We can't trust him.'

'We don't need to; we just need to let him lead us. If he flees, he'll be arrested or shot on sight.'

'Is Jared there? Let me talk to him.'

'He's surveillance, as he'll remain.'

Delphi was at the ticket machine and looked back towards the other end of the hall, to the shadows by the statue, at Lior. Two single tickets to Kiev were ready to be confirmed. 'I've been trying to get to Gabriel for seven years now,' she said, breaking the silence, 'and we're not going to get another chance like this. If Gabriel is capable of shutting down an entire military complex this is game changing. We need to find out who did this, and we need to do it before the entire country is brought to a halt and thousands die.'

'Russia will –' He stopped. There was a second or two of silence. She could hear faint scratching down the line. Then, 'Alright, do it. I need to make a call.'

Delphi had neglected to tell Edward what Lior had said about the code being uploaded to his wetware port. Mentioning it could have pulled the plug until he knew more, which put the whole operation at risk. No, the power to shut down national infrastructures was enough existential risk to give her the greenlight. And if the code capable of doing so was now in Lior's head then how else might he use it? The thought was truly frightening, and she had the uneasy feeling that she was walking towards someone who could pose the largest single threat to human life as she knew it. A kid with nothing but the clothes on his back and a fake passport.

Delphi motioned for Lior to follow her with a flick of her head. He stepped out from beside the column, his eyes on the back of her midnight hair as she moved through the crowds.

'Where's my ticket?' he said, once he had caught up with her.

'I'll keep everything together – pretend we're a couple. Less suspicious that way.'

'No, you're not coming with me.'

She rolled her eyes. 'If the authorities have confirmed your IP address and where you live, they'll already be at mine. What would you like me to do?' Cogs whirred behind his grey irises like sheet lightening, and eventually he looked up with a thousand yard stare through security.

She took his arm. 'Try to look pleased to see me.'

They were making their way through passport control when police burst into the entrance hall. Lior handed over his Lithuanian passport to a stately immigration officer. The police raced through the milling tourists and suits, their black jackets swishing through the air above spit-polished shoes tapping the marble floor.

Whilst he waited for the criminal and civil charges check to finish, the immigration officer studied the passport, pouring over the detail, the photo, the name. He glanced up at Lior, and then back at the photo. Lior could feel a wave of anxiety sweep through him.

The police approached the queues. 'Out of the way,' one of them called out to a group of business people filing across the walkway, wheeling their travel cases behind them. When the first officer burst through the middle of them, Jared appeared. Spinning around into their path he flashed up his ID and said: 'This suspect is now under the protection of the Secret Intelligence Service. This information is classified as secret and if it is leaked I'll have each of you charged under the Official Secrets Act, your presence here having been captured on closed circuit cameras, and my voice recorded on concealed devices on my person. Do you understand?'

They looked at each other briefly, but then nodded.

Jared turned back and re-joined the queue. The wild eyes of passengers shot between them, and whispers circulated in the close vicinity. But as the police moved away and took out their radios to report back to their superiors, people had no option but to get on with their day.

The immigration officer finally passed Lior back the passport and looked between him and Delphi. 'Have a nice trip,' he said, smiling sincerely.

Lior exaggerated his softened accent. 'I'm sure we will.' Then he walked through the gates, a weight lifting from his shoulders.

Jared sunk back into the crowd shuffling towards the trains. He tipped his head to his chest. 'Stand the police down. We've got this.'

This had taken an unexpected turn, but no matter. It was a final chance to cement his operational competence, securing as a consequence a job upstairs and a little stability. A nice house in Putney maybe, somewhere away from the riff-raff. A dog. Some kids to carry on his family name. Delphi would soon come running back, especially if he helped her shine now. A few drinks after a successful op, a little praise here, a promotion there … they'd be giddy with it all. Unstoppable. In love again. It just hinged on this man Gabriel. Find him and get him to UK soil. The rest would follow.

CHAPTER NINE

In the train, Lior rubbed his head in discomfort, feeling drained again. He needed fuel. Delphi leant over the table between them and touched his forearm. Her hands were cold. 'Are you OK?'

'I'd been unconscious since Vosinsk,' he said, raising his head groggily. 'I came out of it this morning with the nastiest hangover of my life, even worse than when I drunk grappa until dawn with a friend and his father the night before he deployed to Chechnya.'

She looked away, out of the window. Her piercing eyes suddenly seemed soft, as if her mask had dropped, and she caught her breath. But they hardened before she replied, 'Can you ...' – she groped for the word and then seemed to make do – '*feel* it inside you, in your head?'

'All I know is that I swing between feeling terrible and being wired. Like my senses are sharper, thoughts quicker.' It was true: he'd been picking out details in the crowd within milliseconds. He anticipated collisions seconds before they took place. Was able with a glance to count the number of pigeons in flight within the station.

Delphi thought for a few moments, then said, 'Did anything else happen that night? Did you take anything?'

'I went home. What did you do?'

'Same as you.'

'I thought you might have caught up with some friends,'

he said. 'Been to a club. I don't know.'

'I would have invited you if I had.'

He smiled. 'We should have just gone ourselves.'

'I don't dance,' she said, raising an eyebrow and pursing her lips. 'I presume that you don't either.'

'I enjoy the atmosphere. Sometimes. It depends who I'm with.'

'Me too.' Her lips stayed closed but dimples formed in her cheeks, and her eyes smiled back.

They each turned away and were quiet for a while, watching other passengers board the train.

Then Delphi whispered, 'You never introduced me you know.'

'I didn't find out how you did on my test.'

'Well, it's too late not to trust me now.'

'I try not to trust anyone.'

She was quiet for a moment, then said, 'The strongest man in the world is the man who stands most alone, right?'

'Something like that.'

'You don't even trust Gabriel? How can you be sure he's created Atma? That it's real?'

'It's not something that can be created fully formed. It's something that evolves, like life.'

'But it's a virtual afterlife? A simulation?'

'It may not exist in space, but to you or me it would seem as real as this moment. As this life. Though this life seems to value work and status at the expense of all else. Don't you agree?'

'Not at all,' Delphi said nonchalantly. 'We have art. We create beauty.'

Lior observed her. He questioned her commitment to his cause. He would have to quickly evaluate her integrity before letting her meet Gabriel. Having excelled during military service and a subsequent deployment to the eastern provinces as a signals officer he did not take fools gladly, despite the multiple sclerosis now eating away at his nervous system. Or else, Lior must convince her of the absolute merit of his endeavour.

'But beauty is being eroded,' Lior responded, flicking the end of his nose with his thumb in agitation. 'We purchase and act to maintain status relative to our peers – as inequality continues to grow we must purchase more, and to do so we incur debt. Debt fuels growing inequality, as those who own capital benefit from those who don't. Growing inequality fuels purchases to maintain status, and so on and so on ad infinitum.

'And then to provide some relief from this existence, we placate ourselves with entertainment, with a means of temporary escape that simultaneously instils further desire for status, serving only to tighten a vicious cycle suffocating joy, creativity and compassion from our increasingly sterile civilisation.

'We work more and more, when we could afford to work less and less. If only we were not driven to value ourselves based on how we believe others to perceive us. Where will we end up? A divided society reminiscent of Rome left to crumble under the weight of its own greed, or – and I'm no Marxist – in revolution? Will we leave ourselves with nothing left like the Easter Islanders? Alone in a great expanse, with no food, no shelter, no life raft. Only war.' He sat back. 'No. In Atma it's as if our lives will finally begin, and once you meet Gabriel I'll show you a world beyond your imagination – one day it will be a universe.'

'I take it your life is worth living?' Delphi threw away. She seemed unmoved, as if she thought it verbose and narcissistic social criticism.

'It wasn't …'

'I can't imagine someone with your taste in wine ever lived a life of dearth, Lior.' He noted how Delphi adopted a solemnity. She was mischievous, unpredictable. That added unnecessary uncertainty.

'I spent most of it in care in Ukraine, near the town of Brovary.'

'I should have guessed you were an orphan.'

'Would you have liked to take me under your wing? I'm sorry to disappoint.'

'Then what happened to your parents?'

'My father lectured …'

As Lior spoke these words, he watched as a man familiar to him entered the other end of the carriage and took a seat on the opposite side of the aisle. The man had been observing them in the station when someone else joined him momentarily and they'd exchanged a few remarks. He settled in his seat quickly and looked out of the window. His dark skin was slightly glossy with perspiration. Perhaps he'd lost track of time and had to run to catch the train. Or perhaps he'd been organising a covert intelligence operation via his phone and had to cut it short to make it aboard before they pulled away. Lior's ability to interpret slight protrusions in his jacket as the shape of a pistol in a chest holster strongly suggested the latter.

Lior stared at him, his mind racing, his heart pounding in his chest.

He looked back at Delphi.

She didn't take her eyes from his. 'Anything wrong?' she said. Lior thought he caught a quiver in her voice.

He looked at the man again as he turned from the window and glanced down the aisle, perhaps checking for an attendant. His eyes flicked to Lior's and they locked for a split-second. He was poker-faced. Then he looked away and leant back in his seat. He took out his phone and flicked from one screen to the next.

The train pulled away from the station.

'Lior?' Delphi said.

'Yes?' he replied quietly.

'I was asking about your parents.'

He didn't answer.

He had been such a fool. Of course she was too good to be true. Brilliantly talented, well turned out, an expert hacker, eager to learn, content to help him flee from the security services. Beautiful. His mind too became silent with the hopelessness of where he found himself. What was he thinking?

At least he now knew. At least he had not led them to Gabriel.

He must play it safe. Stay calm and act as though nothing had happened. Wait for the right opportunity.

Eventually he decided that he must say something. He had to keep the game going. After all, when you dance with the devil you wait for the music to stop. So he turned to her, adopting his own sort of solemnity, a quiet intense kind, in which his eyes never strayed from hers and his whisper became coarse and dry, like sand.

'I can remember meeting my mother, I think when I was near nine or ten years old,' he said. 'I'm not sure exactly. She was different to the people who ran the home where I grew up. The nurse told me that she was my mother, although I did not recognise her, and then this woman, she started to cry. A large drop rolled from her cheek and fell to the carpet with a thud. I don't remember her before then.'

Lior looked out of the window, his expression unchanged.

'How old were you when you were left, put in the –'

'I was told later that it was when I was about four years old …' He trailed off, having had enough of talking, and turned his head to watch the changing landscape.

Delphi continued. 'But how could she do that? What about your father?'

Lior didn't respond; his eyes glazed over staring out of the window. An attendant stopped at Lior and Delphi's seats, drawing his consciousness back from the depths of his past. They were asked for their order and Lior looked up at the uniformed man with jaded eyes. Later, when the food arrived, Lior took it from the attendant wordlessly. He started eating, not pausing between mouthfuls, not looking up from his tray. His body fuelling a metamorphosis within.

CHAPTER TEN

They arrived in Berlin at its new maglev train terminal. The next conventional but high-speed train to Kiev was due to leave in thirty minutes and Lior broke the silence by suggesting they make their way straight to the platform. They followed the stream of passengers leaving work, migrants mostly, observed Lior. Migrants fleeing countries ravaged by decade upon decade of civil and expeditionary warfare; that and desertification from global warming. Lior could hear them now, a cacophony of voices at once from the entire hallway. They burst into his consciousness as he shifted his attention from Delphi's gait. Not only was each conversation audible to him, but he could also comprehend every utterance simultaneously.

Just then, one in particular stood out. 'He sat across the carriage from me, that one, there.'

Lior caught a reflection of the witness and questioning police in the dark glasses of a businessman walking past.

His pulse raced. Now or never.

Slipping beneath the dividing rail into a stream of pedestrians travelling in the opposite direction, he rolled across the seven or eight person berth of concourse until he hit the wall. Still rebounding from the impact, he sprinted away from the voice, staying low, nipping in and out of the faceless masses, sliding against the tiles. Past couples holding hands and convoys of suitcases. Sprinting until he had reached the central terminal again. Until he could disappear into the crowd.

Across the hall, he found a door for members of staff, but it wouldn't open in or out. He tried hitting a button on the wall. Nothing.

He looked around, over each shoulder. Behind him and to the right thirty metres, he saw a movement in the crowd, a parting. There wasn't time to reach another exit. He pushed it again, hard. The metal shook, and some of the people walking by looked around. Lior tapped his pockets down liked he'd just lost his key card. A palm hit a metal object inside his jacket.

Of course.

He pulled out his multi-tool and used the small saw to hook the pins and – with a bit of vigour – release the bolt. The door opened and he spun through it before it closed quickly behind him.

A body slammed into the other side of the metal panels and Lior heard a muffled grunt of frustration before he turned and swept away along the sterile corridor, leaving his pursuer behind. A terror filled his entire being: his mind blanked, his heart thumped inside his chest, and his legs tingled unbearably. He ran.

In the hall, Jared smashed his shoulder against the door, but to no avail. A nearby station supervisor in a light-blue mandarin shirt approached. 'What do you think you're doing?' he said.

Jared saw him and whipped out his ID and pistol, barking orders for him to open the door. German police appeared across the hall, at the entrance to the passageway from which

Lior had escaped. They looked around, CCTV and selected feed displayed on the inside of mirrored glasses. Lior's face was beneath the video. The other lens tried in vain to match it to the hundreds of faces before them.

They saw Jared. They saw the gun.

One of them shouted, 'Everybody down,' and the nearest half of the hall looked around then hit the floor. The officer raised his arm and shot at the sky, breaking a shatter-resistant transparent panel into a thousand pieces. Above the echoing gunshot, but muted crowd, 'Stay where you are and put down the weapon,' travelled across marbled surfaces like a directional speaker.

But Jared was already halfway through the door.

He didn't look back.

Lior ran for his life through a maze of hallways. He'd heard the distant gunshot. It chilled him to the core. Hairs stood up over his spine, up his arms. His legs almost gave way and his bowels could have emptied had he not pulled himself together, tightening every muscle to prevent a debilitating fear from causing him to collapse against a wall.

He reached a fork in the corridor and didn't know which way to turn, didn't know where he was going. Didn't know what the hell he had gotten himself into.

Get a grip and think.

Through a narrow window in a side door, he saw a glimpse of what he thought was daylight. Get in a car and drive east, that's all he had to do.

But this door too wouldn't open, and it didn't have a visible lock. Only a slot for an access card and a keypad. It wouldn't give, and the lack of commotion behind him didn't feel right. He'd heard someone on his tail. The smashing of doors, rubber soles thrashing against the tiled floor.

He tried again, twisting the immobile handle as aggressively as he could. But then something happened he couldn't explain: a code appeared on the keypad panel, the light turned green. A lock clicked open, and the door swung forwards under the weight of his arm.

An unseen hand.

He made a dash for it, his feet thundering across the narrowing space before the door out onto the street. Arms pumping oxygen to his lungs. He was meters from the exit.

'Stop or I fire,' roared Jared. He had just caught the unlocked door and now had his pistol trained on Lior.

Lior skidded to a halt, in two minds as to whether to keep running. He was so close to escaping, and a pistol fired from thirty metres or so might miss its target. He looked at the exit, sizing it up, then back at Jared.

'Don't even think about it', Jared said, walking forwards, closing the gap between them.

'You wouldn't shoot me,' Lior responded. 'You need me.'

Jared lowered the pistol. 'I'll take a chance on aiming at your legs.'

Lior dropped his gaze to his feet. He couldn't deny that he was terrified: he felt deathly cold despite being out of breath. He wasn't going anywhere.

Jared increased his pace and approached Lior with aggression. He took Lior's legs from under him with a swift sweeping kick to the back of his knees and a clothesline arm across his chest. Lior went to lash out with a kick to his ribs as he fell, but Jared caught it and punched him in the face.

'Jared, back away,' Delphi was at the door. Her command caught his hand raised in mid-air. He looked around, then back at Lior. Lior pushed himself to his feet and stepped back into a crouch against the wall. Drawing on grating breath, he gazed at Jared's red fist and then over at two individuals behind Delphi. Berlin Police. They looked at him and stepped forwards.

Delphi raised a hand parallel to the ground, turned and said patiently, 'Please, we need somewhere out of sight for a few minutes.' She was calm and controlled on the surface, like a frozen river. 'This is an important case. We can't afford for it to be compromised.' She paused. 'Can we, Lior?'

He was propped up on an elbow, his cheek red, blood sweeping through a split. His ear was swollen and ringing like a round had been fired next to his head, and he tasted damaged coppery tissue in his mouth. But he just stared back at her and replied, 'No,' his voice as composed and grainy as ever. 'No, we can't.'

Delphi held his gaze coolly before turning to the police officers now beside her, showing them her ID. 'I apologise for any trouble we've caused.'

'What do you think I should be saying to my boss?' said the one closest, thick arms crossed over his tunic.

Jared stood and looked them up and down, his irritation rising. 'Tell them the intelligence services are dealing with it,' he snapped.

There was a movement on the floor. Lior shuffled his feet beneath him. He said, 'Give us ten minutes then report' – he used a knee to launch himself to standing – 'that a suspect has been apprehended and removed from your jurisdiction. We'll be on our way.'

The officer looked him up and down. Lior's crooked smile revealed blood between a canine and incisor. Play ball, he thought.

The officer's arms unfolded. 'Have you got diplomatic clearance for this?'

'Excuse me?' Jared said, stepping towards them.

'Yes,' Delphi said, blocking Jared off and eyeing them with a knowing smile.

The German officer raised his hands. 'Well OK then.' He looked between the three of them, and then over his shoulder at his junior, his eyebrows raised. 'Follow me.'

They were in some staff toilets, Lior leaning over cloudy red water in a hand basin, dabbing his rapidly bruising cheek with a folded tissue in the mirror. He could smell the iron from his blood and acrid bleach. Jared was at another basin, the furthest from Lior's, running cold water over his knuckle whilst watching Delphi. Delphi paced over faded green titles in front of a row of old cubicles. A neo-fascist had drawn a Celtic cross in black permanent marker on the side of the end panel.

'I don't give a damn if you think you've been betrayed, if you think you don't owe us anything, if you think you can make this journey on your own.' Her voice echoed from the hard walls; the acoustics made it deeper, more resonant. It whipped across the space towards Lior.

'Because you will *not* make it. Do I make myself clear?' She glared at his grey eyes in the soiled mirror. But he didn't say anything. He didn't have the chance anyway. 'From now on you will not be free from surveillance, and if you flee you will be shot on sight, then likely repatriated. The Russians no doubt would make sure you reach them eventually.'

Jared dried his hand with paper towels.

'You wouldn't have been able to leave the UK alone,'

Delphi continued, 'so you can drop any resentment. Your attitude. We're going to help you, and you're going to help us. Because we both want the same thing: Gabriel.'

'I don't think I've been betrayed,' Lior said. He splashed water over his face.

'What?'

He snatched a hand towel from the dispenser and ran it over his broken skin. 'Betrayed. I didn't have a choice, as you say.' He started to walk slowly towards Delphi, clipping the tiles with his thin boots. Jared watched him carefully.

'But I don't owe you anything. I know you're not interested in me.' He was impassive. 'So let's keep it strictly business. Let me meet with Gabriel. Let me deal with what I need to deal with. Then he's yours.'

'You'll be wired and tracked.'

'Would you shoot me if I ran?'

'It would be my pleasure,' said Jared, before Delphi could answer. Lior glared and stepped towards him.

She said, 'You're an intelligent man, Lior –'

'Don't patronise me.'

'I mean it. So why run? You must have known you wouldn't make it. If you already knew I was a –'

Lior cut her off. 'A spook? I was recognised by a woman being shown a police photo of me. She was pointing me out. You spoke to the police, you knew they were looking for me.'

Delphi looked at Jared and said quietly, 'Who would have done that?'

'The Met police,' he replied. 'They'd have alerted Paris, Brussels and Berlin directly in minutes. Any city that a train from London stops at. Then Europol.'

'But who would have told the Met but not Border Force?'

Jared looked at her. Cogs turning over. 'We'll talk about

that.'

Lior glanced between Delphi and Jared. Something wasn't right.

'How long 'til the next train?' Delphi said, changing the subject.

Lior replied without looking at his watch. 'Six minutes.'

'Jolly good,' said Jared. 'We're getting on it.'

'Lior,' Delphi snapped, 'follow me, but now you'll have an advanced close-protection-trained intelligence officer and a 9 mm at your back. Let's go.' Jared grinned at Lior.

Lior drew his lips tight, weighing up his options. It didn't take long. He stepped towards Delphi, prompting her to turn and walk away. Jared studied her, leaning casually on the washbasin. He looked impressed, but in a bemused sort of way, and as if he wanted her to know it. But she didn't meet his eyes.

Lior tailed Delphi. He saw the way she ignored Jared. He saw the hint of something that was more than professional veneration from him, something deeper, and judging by an edge to his slit eyes, something darker. Eventually, Jared moved from a slouch to standing, pushing off the side of the basin. He shadowed Lior. Lior could feel faint breath on the back of his neck, and smell fresh sweat.

He didn't trust either of them, but particularly Jared. He was a man who knew the law to the letter, but then broke it anyway.

CHAPTER ELEVEN

It was dusk. The sky was overcast, bleak; trees stood leafless like etchings against it.

In the unpeopled carriage, Lior was sleeping, his head lolling against the inside of the padded rest, his eyelids fluttering. Across the aisle, Jared took a seat opposite Delphi. With her eyes on his, she could also keep Lior's dark shape in her periphery.

'The Russian's are getting uneasy about the little given away so far, despite news of Lior,' Jared said.

'We've got time though, haven't we?' Her eyes flicked to his.

'Not much. The President gave a speech half an hour ago. Threw people into a bit of a panic.'

'They sending anyone over?'

'By the sound of it.'

Delphi sighed and looked over at Lior to check he was sleeping. He was motionless, and she looked back at Jared. 'Why do the Russians know Lior left the UK? Why does anyone know?'

Jared leant forwards, his eyes fixed on hers. 'Edward wants to know too.' He let her mull that over – the ramifications were significant. Her eyes were impassive but an intelligence raced behind them.

There was only one way it made sense. Someone wanted the Russians to know. Someone in the team. Someone wanted

Lior locked away without concern for the larger implications. Or worse, they welcomed them. And that someone had made himself or herself known. This was a big hand to play now.

The train swayed back and forth a few times as they crossed tracks. Then Jared said, 'I've missed working with you, you know.'

Delphi's voice was flat, her eyes levelled at him as she replied. 'I think I'll sign off after this op.' She looked out into the night. 'Do something completely different.'

Jared studied her face in silence then glanced at Lior.

'You know, if this goes well, I'll probably be deputising for Edward. That leaves a gap open.'

'I'm serious.'

'Well, if you need a place to stay, to get something new off the ground you know where I am.'

'What about your sister?'

'She's …' Jared looked away then down at his clasped hands. 'She's still in a bad way.'

Delphi's face dropped. 'Still at the clinic?'

He hesitated, then cupped his palms over his face and said, 'She won't leave there now.'

She touched his forearm. 'I'm sorry, Jared.'

'It's fine,' he replied, pulling his fingers over the corners of his eyes, 'I should have done more … but it's fine, she should have called me –'

'You've been away.'

'I know,' Jared said. He stared up at the ceiling, his head tilted back against the rest. After a minute or so he looked back at her and broke the silence. 'What's the next chapter for you?'

'Not sure. I just know that I'm not interested in becoming the next Edward. Though I feel sorry for him.'

Jared seemed to mull this over. 'He's only got himself to blame though, you know,' he said eventually. 'He was in above his head.'

Delphi went back to looking out the window. 'Do you think the Borschevsky family is still after him? I would have thought that he's suffered enough, more than they intended. But you never know.'

'If there was an assessed threat he'd still have protection twenty-four seven.'

Delphi's eyes lost focus and her cheeks blood, so that as she gazed out of the window again, Jared said, 'Delphi, you're not a target, do you hear me? They wouldn't know you were supporting him. And even if they did, they've had their reprisal, it's finished.'

'Maybe, you're right,' she said not turning to face him. 'But sometimes I wonder why Edward pushed Artem as hard as he did. Why take that risk?'

'Arrogance. And he's good at his job, though we both know he wouldn't risk life and limb for anyone. Which is why Artem died and took others with him. It's why he's head of cyber at thirty-eight.'

'We're all made of crooked timber really.'

'Hence we have a job.'

On the other side of the carriage, Lior's eyes became slits and he watched Delphi shuffle back in her seat, glancing birdlike down and away in what betrayed either nerves or agitation. Then she looked out through windows that reflected her motionless features, her eyes softened by the past.

Jared said, 'Although some of us are more crooked than others,' and flicked his head in Lior's direction.

'Maybe,' Delphi responded, not moving.

Jared lowered his voice. 'What do you think of this kid, anyway?'

'I don't know. Now he seems terrified, and then he appears to know much more than he's giving away. Before … he was, well, he was thoughtful, interesting. Interesting to talk to.'

'How often did you do that?'

'At first just the usual snippets, and then after a few months, up until we met, we'd message each other every couple of nights.'

'How'd you reel him in?'

'Just the usual.' She shrugged her shoulders.

'There's no such thing.'

'I don't know, Jared. We like reading a lot of the same books, Philip K Dick, Neuromancer, stuff like that. We'd discuss hacks and debugging issues, what other people were up to.'

'Anything else?'

Delphi said quietly, 'Not really.'

Jared rubbed the stubble on his chin with the palm of his hand, watching her. 'Doesn't sound that interesting to me,' he said, not taking his eyes from hers.

Delphi stared back at him – one side of her nose crinkled – then raised her eyebrows and looked back out of the window.

'We should have just blackmailed him you know, like a normal suspect, instead of treating him to a trip across Europe.'

'He wouldn't have given us anything. And why break our cover when we both wanted the same thing? It was a risk, but Gabriel is worth taking a risk on. And we're still on route.'

'For now.'

Delphi let her head loll back between the headrest and glass and closed her eyes. 'I'm going to sleep.'

Jared watched her, his expression unreadable. Except for what Lior thought was a momentary flicker of resentment, touched by something else. Guilt maybe.

It was the dead of night and through the window Lior observed dark empty landscapes sweep past in an eerie silence. He thought about Gabriel, he thought about finding him that first time, soon after he had first been able to travel alone. He remembered making his way down the long, high corridor, over creaking, narrow floorboards. Finding the name engraved on a great hardwood door at the very end of an otherwise empty wing of the building.

He knocked tentatively and then pushed it open with two hands. He was small and malnourished and the door was heavy. He told the professor that his mother, Anna Meyer, was very sick and needed help. Standing there in the doorway, his arms by his side. A soldier. The man's face grew and before Lior could run a bony hand had gripped his arm and yanked him backwards through the door. It slammed with an almighty crack, drawing prickly tears from his young eyes.

'Why are you still awake?' Lior looked around to meet Delphi's half-closed eyes watching him from above a grey blanket pulled up to her cheeks. Jared was asleep opposite her.

Lior said quietly, 'When my mother died someone in the care home told me, 'Not to worry, she's only asleep. It's just that now she will never wake up.''

'You don't expect me to still believe that crap do you?'

Lior turned back to the window.

Minutes had passed when, without looking away from the distant settlements, he said, 'Do you hate me for what I have done?'

'Hate's a strong word.'

'I don't care,' he said, looking dead at her.

'What do you care about?'

'My survival,' he stated. 'And my parents.'

'You're right, maybe I do hate you.' She was seemingly nonchalant. 'But I hate the man you work for more.'

'There's nothing wrong in self-interest. You claim to defend civilisation and yet seemingly despise that which has made it great.'

'What possible benefits have your or his actions given society?'

'Remind me of what that is again: society? I see only a mass of dispirit individuals striving for worth and significance, trudging to places of work for fifty years then being left to die alone in empty homes. They can go anywhere they want, speak to anyone on the planet in seconds, order goods from every company, or even print them in their own homes. *If* they have the credit. What society are they part of? What does 'society' offer them compared to what awaits, when Gabriel's self-interest leads these individuals in their last days to a better life than they had ever even hoped for in their most reckless moments of aspiration? And all of this is hidden. All of this is repressed, and yet so close.'

'Everyone would be infinitely better off if governments just got out of the way, right? Who needs police or the armed forces? You can clearly look after yourself.'

'Everything has been accounted for.'

'Are you saying you will protect Gabriel?'

'No, I'm saying you should.'

'Otherwise you won't be able to have him help you, to extract the virus? You won't be able to upload? You'll be left behind. One of the downtrodden masses.'

'I need to know whether he can help me.' He could see her wanting to ask a question but then stop herself. Perhaps she wondered why Gabriel would set up the cyber-attack, frame someone for it, and then want to help that very same person. It didn't make sense. Which is why it couldn't have happened. He also knew that Gabriel wouldn't have wanted to corrupt Vosinsk's supercomputer. It wasn't intentional, something had gone wrong. It was a mistake.

Unless other agencies were at work.

She wanted Gabriel. But he knew that what she really wanted wouldn't stop at him. No matter: with providence, he'd get the code removed. No one else alive would be able to, he knew that much, if Gabriel himself could not.

Then he'd disappear.

CHAPTER TWELVE

They arrived in Kiev. Lior was bugged and left to find Gabriel, as agreed. After taking a convoluted route through town he left the subway close to Pushkin Park. He walked from there to the National Technical University of Ukraine. It was the midday break and amidst a scattering of students with his head down against the cold drizzle he could move unnoticed amongst the crowd. But that didn't stop him walking into the side of a man drawing on a cigarette on the main path beneath the branches of a pine. Lior spun around and threw an apology back without stopping.

With his eyes again on the hefty main door, his feet strode purposefully and within a few paces reciprocal insults muttered under smoke-filled breath were out of earshot. Stomping up the steps, Lior took the man's wallet from his inside pocket and used one of the cards to swipe through the barriers in the entrance. The wet soles of his boots slapped against the marble floor. Then up familiar steps to the third storey. Once there he headed east to a wing in the far corner of the building.

Professor Isimov's office hadn't moved from the labs at the end of a long corridor, cut off from the bustle of the central halls and lecture theatres. He'd obviously dug himself in over the last few years. Lior took a deep breath and knocked twice.

'Vstoupit,' was barked from a muffled distance. Lior

creaked open the door. Sweat had created a film over his palms. He could have been that small boy all over again.

Through the gloom he could make out a withered man sitting at a large desk at the far end. His wiry grey hair was more dishevelled than he remembered. His skin oily and pale. But his eyes were alive, consumed by a tablet in front of him, a point scribbling away at algorithms too complex to be directed by way of his wetchip alone. A diagram of what looked like a computer system was on one side of the screen. Components were added to it following the completion of each section of code.

He didn't look up.

Lior took measured steps towards the desk, his eyes fixed on the old man's forehead. Dark bushy eyebrows danced beneath it. The room was dim. Black blinds clung to towering window frames, the hum of machines droned through the dry air and sapped the saliva from his mouth. Six feet from the desk, Lior stopped, the sound of his boots on the wooden floor dissipating, allowing the buzzing to heighten like cicadas at nightfall.

Eventually, he said one word: 'Gabriel.'

Without stopping, Professor Isimov spoke heavy, rolling Ukrainian. 'You have the wrong person.'

There was silence as a nervousness rushed through Lior, his legs becoming weak in the face of the authority that this man commanded.

'It's me, professor. Tomas,' he said eventually in a Ukrainian that trembled slightly, that was more anglicised. At that, the professor calmly stopped working, his expression unchanged. And then his eyes shot up at Lior's. He studied him, looking over his features. The thick eyebrows descending over squinting, beady eyes. His mouth curled in apparent disgust or, at least, distaste.

And then, just as calmly as he had stopped, he looked down and continued with his work. A full minute could have passed.

'What do you want?' he said frankly, all hesitancy gone, along with the stuffy professor façade.

'I take it you've heard about Vosinsk?'

'I have heard.'

Lior waited.

Eventually, 'What happened?'

'A virus happened.'

Gabriel paused and then said in monotone, 'You shouldn't have come here.'

'Did you make it?'

'No. I know nothing of it. All I know is that you have failed. And that you are now on the run, so let me say it again, you shouldn't have come here. In fact, you must leave. Now.'

'Whatever it was, it jumped into my wetchip. And I went somewhere, in my mind. There was a figure walking towards me. Warning me.'

Gabriel's eyes narrowed.

'I was out cold for days afterwards. And now things have happened. I don't need my glasses anymore, memories are firing all over the place, and I feel like something is growing inside of me, along my nerves. It's burning –'

'How could someone program a virus to upload to the wetchips? There just hasn't been the time, or the exposure.'

'How could they create a virus that shut down an entire military station in seconds? If something went wrong, I need to know.' Lior felt a lump rise in his throat. 'I need your' – his voice broke – 'I need your help.'

'I will not say it again; there's nothing I can do. If I do

not know what happened, I can't help you. Now get out.'

A floorboard creaked outside the door. Gabriel watched as shadows played out beneath it. Then they stopped.

'Hello?' called the professor. But there was no reply. 'Did anyone follow you here?'

Lior froze, and then to his horror Gabriel calmly pulled open a drawer beside him and took out a pistol. He inserted a magazine and held it at his waist, aimed towards the door. Lior had suspected that when Gabriel was a signals officer he had been seconded to Ukrainian Special Forces. The mention of having been on operations in Donetsk was enough. Right then, as his heart thumped in his chest, he'd have bet his life on it.

Lior stepped away from the centre of the room just as the brass doorknob began to turn. Like a knee jerk reaction he said in English with some force, 'I don't know who it is, why don't you put the gun away.'

The knob instantly stopped turning.

Gabriel turned the gun on Lior. He released the safety with his thumb. He shook with a fury that threatened to clench the trigger at any moment. Lior watched the muscles in his fingers contract. He felt his own body go limp, his legs turned to lead as he faced death. In desperation, he looked into the old man's eyes. He looked for a hint of the past, for any approval, for a connection crossing barriers they had each constructed.

He didn't see anything of the sort.

But Gabriel eventually took a much-needed breath and his anger seemed to subside.

'When I first looked upon you,' he said, 'I knew you were Anna's boy.' Lior's hair stood on end. 'Why did you not come back?'

'I was afraid.'

Gabriel let his head drop, in shame, thought Lior. The old man fiddled with the pistol in his lap, clicking the safety catch back on. Then he looked up. His eyes were encircled by pink fatigued lids sagging with their weight.

'So was I,' he said, eventually. He rested the gun on the desk in front of him then looked down at his hands. 'I always have been.'

Lior stared at him in disbelief. Could this be what he had longed for all his life? For this man to recognise him as his son.

Crack. The door flew open whistling around on its hinges and ricocheted off the wall. Jared shot forward, his pistol held steady, aimed at Gabriel. With the door closing behind him, he barked, 'Stay where you –'

But before he could finish, Gabriel grasped his handgun. Jared's eyes narrowed and he began to step to one side.

Bang.

Jared fired first. Gabriel slumped in his seat clutching his arm and fired a succession of shots back.

Bullets flew past Jared, splintering the hardwood-clad walls as he spun behind a steel rack of computer equipment. He fired shot after shot at the professor. A bullet hit the light switch causing deep shadows to leap across the hardwood furniture and computer equipment. Between them, narrow shafts of sunlight cut through gaps in the blinds, brightening the gloom above complete darkness. Jared thumped into the side of the rack and sunk to a squat beneath Gabriel's line of fire.

Three steady shots punctured just above his head and then stopped. He counted to five, his lips moving silently.

He had Delphi in his ear. 'Jared, sitrep.'

76

Jared whispered into his collar. 'Get here now. Kiev Tech, east wing, third floor.'

Then with his little finger he pulled the tiny earpiece out from behind the fold in his ear and tucked it into his pocket. He needed to concentrate.

After a second of quiet in which the ringing permeated throughout the room, Jared crept alongside the shelving to a gap. He paused for a heartbeat and then swung the weapon around to the desk. But it was only an emptiness of broken shapes of greys and black.

Nor was there sign of Lior.

Then a swish of movement passed over the end of the shelving at the other side of the room, and a side door clicked open. Jared stalked across the floorboards, his body low, the pistol an extension of his wrist.

He reached the edge of the doorway, his back to the wall, and again looked for Lior. The main door had swung shut so he must still be in the room. Jared twisted around to the adjacent door, straining to get one eye on the length of the corridor behind him.

Bang. A bullet whizzed past his face and punctured the far wall. He threw himself back against the wooden cladding. This had got out of control. He needed to rescue the situation fast.

'Gabriel', he shouted, 'why don't you put down your weapon and speak to me before the police arrive? There are things we need to discuss.'

Jared waited, the pad of his thumb stroking the pistol's grip. He glanced back through the door quickly, but was again greeted by a bullet that this time ripped through the doorframe and slashed through his deltoid. He grunted in pain as his opposite hand went to the stinging wound, and he rolled away from the darkness beside him.

'Discuss that,' Gabriel barked from the corridor.

'Damn you', Jared raged, and he threw a succession of shots back at him. Bang-bang-bang. The ringing faded. 'We know what you're up to, you pathetic parasite.'

The lack of reply almost made Jared turn back towards the door, but then it came, stopping him.

'What am I up to? What do you presume to know?'

'Why don't you accompany me to The Hague and explain for yourself? Or am I better off speaking to the Kremlin?' Jared clutched his shoulder and winced in pain.

'It sounds like you should speak to some of my students.'

'Why? Are there others like Lior?'

'That boy is nothing.'

'Because he screwed up?'

From the other end of the room, the still hidden Lior screamed: 'I told you I didn't.' His voice echoed in the darkness.

'You let them take the risks, is that it?' Jared said.

'He wanted to,' responded Gabriel. 'He made all the effort.'

'Why would he do that? Why did you do that, Lior? Why help this old man screw you?'

'You are the one who has left me with no choice but to pull the plug,' Gabriel said. 'It is on your head. Who sent you? Are you SAS? MI6?'

'Lior led us. Your own protégé.'

There was a silence.

And then a desperate Lior exploded from the darkness. 'I had no choice – I need someone to *help* me.' His rage was guttural and raw. 'I haven't done anything, I didn't mean to kill anyone.'

From through the closed door, footsteps could be heard thundering like an approaching storm at the end of the hall. In desperation, Gabriel fired at the edge of the doorway again, towards Jared. Bullets slammed against wooden panels and walls hidden in the gloom.

Lior flinched in fear as plaster fell over him. Then, as he glanced over his shoulder towards the heavy door, time seemed to slow. Boots kicked through the wood. Diffused sunlight burst from the doorway into the room over Jared. He dropped his pistol and stood with his good arm raised and the other bent upwards from the elbow. Armed police in body armour and helmets thundered throughout the open-plan labs. Ducking behind worktops and desks. Metal pinging off metal above them.

Gabriel had made his way to a side door, and with his old but steady hand, threw quick shots – one more into the side of Jared and then two through the closest balaclavas. The returning ferocity of fire shattered the doorway and Gabriel spun and disappeared through it.

When the automatic rifles were lowered, two policemen lay dead, but the hall within which Gabriel had hidden was clear. Jared shuffled back against the wall as wiry police officers took up positions around him and then filed quietly through the door, keeping low.

Shots were fired from the other end of the corridor, a stray bullet hitting a policewoman about to enter. On either side the others were forced to lie in wait. Another officer pulled the casualty across the floor, out of the line of fire. Cries of pain and rapid commands filled the air in between the cracks of bullets. Smoke and dust scattered.

Amid the hive of rushing bodies and sprawling computer shelving, Jared was on the verge of losing consciousness lying against a wall, blood seeping from his abdomen over the floorboards. But through his yellowing and blurred vision, he could just make out Lior dragging the lifeless body of an armed policeman through the door of a store cupboard on the far side of the room. Even if anyone had paid any attention to him in those few moments, Jared would have been too feeble to let them know.

CHAPTER THIRTEEN

Delphi eventually caught up with the taxi that had supposedly carried Lior. She found it empty, apart from the tracking chip stuffed down the side of the back seat. And now sitting there in the back of the unmanned vehicle, damp with the rain, she watched as the droplets turned to sleet, then light flecks of snow. He'd given them the slip, as Jared had predicted. Jared had followed Lior whilst Delphi trusted that he would comply with their arrangement. She'd trusted him for a reason she could not comprehend.

Eventually the taxi turned off a main road and made a smooth left, then a right past the wide lawns surrounding the imposing university building. Delphi could see a crowd at the head of a path that led up to the entrance, halfway down the street. Police vans, ambulances, tape cutting off the road. She got out and ran. The light snow had turned to large flakes and whipped passed her.

She slowed to a walk when a gaunt looking policewoman motioned for her to turn back. Stretchered casualties were being brought out of the main entrance then along the path to the road and into the hands of the waiting paramedics. Delphi pulled out her phone, started a voice recording and asked her what had happened like an eager journalist.

'Move away,' the policewoman said in her native Ukrainian, the large pupils in her deep-set eyes fixing Delphi like bottomless pits. 'We'll make statement later.'

'Who are the casualties?' Delphi shot back in Russian. Whilst waiting for a reply she strained to see over her to find Jared or Lior's face amongst them.

'The families will be told,' said the policewoman, switching to Russian. 'Then we will tell you. Now leave.' But at that moment she was called over by a superior and so strolled back to the jigsaw of ambulances and police vehicles by the entrance to the path.

Delphi continued watching and was joined by onlookers. Small crowds of people who had been passing by were forming at either end of the taped-off street.

Then she saw him. Jared. On a stretcher being loaded into the back of an ambulance. His eyes closed and features bloodied and limp. Delphi's face dropped. Already pale in the wintry air, it now turned translucent.

'Oh God,' she whispered, her mouth left open. He was a bastard, but he didn't deserve this. Not death. Not now. Neither did Lior. But where was he? And what the hell had happened inside? In the depths of the university. Where supple minds are nurtured and ambitions built.

When no more casualties emerged from between the large ornate entrance doors, Delphi eventually drifted away from the scene. She turned and stepped quietly along a pavement beside the university grounds. She played possible events over in her mind. Lior didn't have any weapons and was unlikely to have obtained one himself. Unless he'd had one hidden, perhaps in an old classroom beneath a floorboard.

She hadn't thought of that.

But he just wanted help. If Gabriel couldn't provide it, maybe Lior had turned on him, then shot Jared and the police sent to stop him. Another possibility was that Gabriel had the weapon. It made more sense, it was his patch and he had more to protect. Jared arriving could have set it all off.

Whatever had happened, Lior was not one of the injured. He could be one of the dead, probably being laid out along a corridor away from cameras and the general public. He could have been arrested and was currently being held inside.

The other possibility was that he had escaped.

If he was under arrest or dead then in all likelihood she would not be seeing him again outside of a courtroom or body bag. If he was alive, however, she needed to find him.

It could now be her only constructive action: apprehending him making an escape. Quickening her pace, she turned a corner onto a smaller side road, still tracing the edge of the university lawns. She searched the distant line of parked cars and front courtyards of well-kept, stone terraced properties facing the campus. The day had darkened with heavy clouds and a low sun, and the end of the road was difficult to make out. But she thought she could see a distant figure in black. It came in and out of focus, sometimes crossing behind parked cars and old payphone boxes. The figure seemed to be moving with some discomfort, one leg carrying most of the weight.

Delphi crossed the street, to the opposite side of the apparition, stooping behind the cars. Then she broke into a sprint.

In the black outfit of an armed police officer, Lior whipped down marble stairs – tripping on one of them as he passed the first floor – crashing from one wall to another, and then burst through a fire escape and out onto the street. At one end, emergency services flew along the adjacent road visible between governmental buildings, startling pedestrians as they stopped to look back towards the main entrance to the university.

Lior turned and forced himself away, he had a small limp – a sprained ankle – that caused him to step up on the ball of that foot and draw breath between closed teeth. But he kept moving.

He didn't really know what for, where could he go now? He'd have to run. Or hide. But neither option brought him any closer to finding help. Why did I let them follow me? he demanded of himself, sickened at his own actions. But what choice did he have? Arrest and repatriation to Ukraine or Russia? Fleeing Kiev whilst trailed by the Russian security services? Defection? He had to get to the one man he thought could help him, and in his mind he did so without a tail.

He was broken, his thoughts scattered but firing away like an Uzi. Calculations of integers, prime numbers and ratios playing out deep within his mind. Sights and sounds of sitting on the upper deck of a London bus sprang up like a memory – but not one that seemed in any way familiar. In it, he stared out of the window, his eyes drawn to the top of the BT Tower on Wentworth Street, its dishes and aerials puncturing the pale overcast sky. The bus rattled along beneath it, and his eyes followed, transfixed, analysing each panel, each strut, each dish. His gaze eventually settled on the highest roof, dominated by a spire in its centre, thrust upwards towards the heavens.

Then a blast shook the ground beneath his feet.

The shock wave roared through the air, ripping its very fabric in a crack that left Lior's ears buzzing with a sharp squeal. Looking back at the university, it was clear a large section on the opposite side had collapsed. He could see the rubble through windows beside him, rubble that filled half of what had been a courtyard in the middle of the U-shaped complex. The wing where he had been only minutes before had seemingly slumped into it. Glass windows burst outwards. Thick smoke and dust was billowing up into the sky and fires had caught where gas pipes had ruptured. Screams quickly echoed from within the gardens, filtering out over the rooftops.

For a moment Lior stood to the spot, stunned, his face contorted from the sudden fear. It only slowly became relief that he had escaped. Relief overshadowed by the hopelessness facing him now that not only had Gabriel been supposedly ignorant of his affliction but – having let himself be cornered within the labs – was now unquestionably dead. The man for whom life was that which must resist death, perpetually in his case. A man Lior longed for recognition from, longed for reward. If the infection by a devastating code was it, then he took its significance to his fiery grave.

And now all that was left was the source.

A silver Tesla sedan turned onto the street without a sound, as if a cat edging towards its prey, then stopped in the middle of the road. There was no other traffic. A dressed-up elderly couple, probably on their way to a pre-theatre dinner, sat in the front aghast at the scene of an explosion in front of them. They hadn't seen Lior.

The man – the driver – stepped out and stood behind his door appalled at what he was seeing across the roof of his car. His wife was screaming at him to get back in, groping at the hem of his navy blazer.

Then she saw Lior.

Losing a second's hesitation to shock, but only one

second, Lior had started to cross the street. The woman looked at him, at the dishevelled militant-looking police officer, her mouth still slack, her eyes alight with flames and smoke. She was frozen in fear.

'Step away from the car,' Lior roared in Ukrainian. 'You will find it at the central police station tomorrow morning.'

The man jolted, looked Lior up and down. He was confounded, petrified, tried to speak but couldn't. He took a shove in the chest with an open palm to clear from the door. It was as Lior dropped onto the seat and reached to pull the door closed, as the woman screamed and fumbled out of her side, that he saw Delphi.

She was dashing towards him, her taut body and pistoning legs only twenty or so meters away. Lior slammed the gearstick into drive and kicked down on the accelerator, sending the tyres spinning over the tarmac, smoking and whining. Suddenly the vehicle was propelled around in a one hundred and eighty-degree spin, arcing away from Delphi, away from the university. The couple rushed aside in opposite directions, the woman tripping over the kerb in her heels.

Delphi's legs continued to thunder into the ground, closing in as the tail end of the car swung around towards her, leaving dark tyre marks in a thin blanket of snow now settling on the freezing rain. The car started to accelerate away, but at the last possible moment she reached out and caught the passenger door handle. The door swung open and she clung to the top of the frame and the roof, her boots dragging over icy slush.

The car braked as they neared the end of the street and she vaulted up and swung her legs in. She grasped the handgrip inside the doorframe, and as the car careened around the corner she was left in a crouch leaning out over the tarmac, her wild, dark hair swept back in a torrent of icy air. On the straight she eventually hit the seat. She pulled the door to and rounded on Lior, as he looked around at her, his eyes wide, arms locked against the wheel.

'Alright, Lior, just take us across town and find a side street.'

'Like hell I will. I should never have trusted you.'

'Jared just saved your life, for the second time.'

'No, he almost got me killed – and now look where things are.' Black smoke still billowed out above the rooftops behind them, and he started to slow the car as they merged with traffic.

'So Gabriel pulled a gun on you?'

His face was hard.

'Lior, we've done everything to facilitate you being here. We've protected you.'

'I should have come alone.'

'That wasn't your choice,' she said. 'Besides, what difference would it have made?' Delphi glanced at the road as they weaved around another car. 'Did he help you?'

Lior stayed silent.

'What did he say? Did he know about it?'

Still nothing.

'If you don't give me anything, I've got no one else but you.'

'No,' he said, his hands clenching the steering wheel. 'He said he didn't know what happened.'

'Do you trust him?'

Lior hesitated, then said, 'I can trust no one else … I *could* trust no one else. It doesn't matter, it's all gone. There's no proof of anything now.'

'We need to get you to the embassy. We can try to help

you from there. We can help build a new life for you.'

'Because he's dead?'

'If he's dead he can't argue his case can he?' she shot back.

Lior's grip on the steering wheel tightened, turning his knuckles white. 'I don't need a new life. I need my old life back.'

'What, no job, no family, no real friends?'

'I had a father,' Lior said, his eyes always on the road, guiding them past cars crawling along the Patona Bridge. They crossed the Dnieper River. It was broad and deep, lights from each bank shimmering on its surface as dusk fell.

'I thought you didn't know him?' Delphi asked.

'Gabriel was my father.' He let the words sink in, work their way into her psyche. Everything up until now had been driven by her desire to find and convict that man. The only family Lior had.

'So now I don't have anyone,' he said. Then he looked at Delphi. 'Just like you.'

She met his gaze for a second and then looked away. He continued, 'I take it you hadn't dug that up?'

'No,' she said softly, 'we hadn't.'

After some time, Delphi turned to Lior. 'I'm sorry.'

'It wasn't you; it was Jared.'

Delphi didn't reply and they drove on in silence past Darnyts'ke cemetery. People in thick winter coats ambled by stark trees. Above them streetlights were starting to flicker into life. The traffic lights ahead were on red and a queue of cars had built up as half the city tried to get home for the evening. They came to a stop and waited.

Delphi turned to Lior. 'When did you find out he was your father?'

'I hacked into Kiev's registry from school. Found a DNA match, did some research on his habits and put two and two together.'

'Your mother never told you?'

'No, I was old enough to shave but that was about it. Not that I let my age stop me from doing other things the establishment thought I shouldn't.' He smiled at her.

She raised one of her narrow eyebrows half-heartedly as if caught somewhere between a schoolmistress and a colleague overhearing one side of a conversation.

They pulled away from the traffic lights and a police car drifted into the lane behind the stolen Tesla. Two male officers stared ahead expressionlessly, and traffic died down around them allowing an eerie tranquillity to descend over the cityscape.

The officer in the passenger seat glanced down at the console on the dash, then looked again the vehicle registration ahead of him. He hit the lights.

CHAPTER FOURTEEN

'Dammit,' Lior hissed. The police car behind him closed the gap and he felt his chest tighten.

Delphi looked over. 'What?'

'Don't turn your head.'

Glancing through her window into the twilight, Delphi could see blue lights licking the wing mirror. She sat back. 'Keep driving.'

Lior pulled out to overtake a white hatchback. A greying lady was hunched over the wheel. But the police edged out from behind her to follow them, out into the centre of the road, coming alongside her wild eyes.

'Stay calm,' Delphi said. 'I'll think of a way out of this.'

But Lior's mind was racing faster than hers – he checked the charge level: it was three-quarters full.

'There's only one.' And then his toes leant on the accelerator with more force, and they started to pull away from their tail.

'No, you're not dragging me into this.'

'Just as you didn't drag me? I'll drop you outside the city.'

'And where will you go?'

'Vosinsk.' He gripped the steering wheel.

'Hold on.' He jerked the wheel around to the right, throwing Delphi against his shoulder. The rear tyres swung around, leaving burnt rubber streaks across the two lanes. He stamped on the accelerator and they rocketed through a full one-eighty turn, narrowly avoiding the lady in the hatchback who, her face twisted in horror, had slammed on the brakes and skidded past them, the two cars missing by inches.

They roared up an access road leaving the police car stranded on the inside lane, trying desperately to cut across the flow of cars. The police eventually pushed through a gap as traffic came to a halt around them and they joined Lior and Delphi on the slip road. Fifty metres or so behind, they hit the siren.

Inside the Tesla, Lior punched zoom-out on the sat-nav display and took a mental photograph of the city's road network.

'You can't just waltz into a Russian military installation. What are you going to do, even if you somehow manage to get there?'

'I need to get this thing out. Somehow. Any way I can. Then I'll disappear. You can pin the blame on Gabriel. Say that I escaped in the blast. Held you at gunpoint.'

'It's suicide.'

'No. All other roads lead to death. I need to get there. He could have made it across.'

'But Atma has gone. It's over, Lior. Finished. It was a pipe dream. This,' she gestured around them with her hand, 'this is real. Conflict is real.'

'This is transitory.'

He spun the car down a side street, roaring downhill between two narrow rows of parked cars. Delphi braced herself against the dashboard.

'I hope you know what you're doing.'

'We did a bit of advanced driving in the army.' His Ukrainian lilt unashamedly crept into his voice. They hit a speed bump at eighty kilometres an hour, ricocheting them both against the roof, hands holding them down as first the front tyres and then the rear took flight. They landed with another heavy thud, fully utilising the car's state-of-the-art suspension.

'I'm so pleased,' Delphi said once she had settled in her seat again.

They flew around a blind corner, scraping a courier's transit van. The Tesla's rear end scratched two lines of paint from the sliding door, before whipping back in line behind the front tyres, powering them against the flow of scattering headlights. Ripping past a scooter, Lior banked into the inside lane and floored it.

The police made the crossroads as Lior whipped around a further corner onto Prazka Street at the opposite end. The stringy officer in the passenger seat had his radio out, barking a request for backup whilst bracing himself against the dashboard. They broke sharply and swerved to avoid a pickup truck pulling out into the road.

Delphi had her phone on her lap.

'What are you doing?'

'Disabling the tracker.'

'You can't hack these things anymore, it takes hours.'

She raised an eyebrow. 'Want to bet?'

She applied her code and a warning light appeared on the car's display screen.

'Done,' she said, slipping her phone into her pocket. Lior smiled broadly, his eyes still on the road. Just then his feet wouldn't have touched it.

Up ahead they were approaching a main highway heading northeast. Lior nipped across a column of cars hogging the inside lane, cutting over the lines, and pulled across in front of the flow of traffic. He took the next junction, pulled into a multi-storey car park beside the flyover, helixed up to the fourth storey, screeched to the end of the row and swung into an empty space bathed in shadows. They sat there in silence, listening. Delphi cast her eyes out over the city, following the dark, winding Dnieper around up-lit gothic spires and squat stone buildings veiled by twilight.

After a number of seconds – and no sign of their tail – Delphi's phone started buzzing. She answered the withheld number and the reply came via the car's speakers, surprising her.

'Delphi, it's Edward. I've spoken to the embassy. Where the hell are you?'

She hesitated, casting a glance at Lior, then tried to delink her phone from the car whilst she answered. 'I pursued Lior escaping the scene –'

'Unity; he's to be referred to by his codename Unity from now on. I swear the list is a bloody joke.' Delphi put her finger to her lips and looked at Lior.

'OK, I pursued Unity – who's sitting next to me now with you on speaker – I'm trying to disconnect the phone. We were initially tailed by local police and have stopped in a car park across town. I was planning to head to the embassy.'

'Forget that. I need you to get to Vosinsk as soon as possible. A Russian delegation was in Kiev this weekend. Over one hundred diplomats and chief execs, including the Russian ambassador, are thought to have been in the conference room directly beside the explosion. The emergency services are just starting to pick bodies out of the rubble.'

'This can't be happening.'

'It is – deal with it. And that's not the worst of it. You've really played a blinder here, Delphi. The Russian's are blaming us.'

'What?'

'I'm sending a team over there now to bring back Jared before they move against him. If they get him we're finished. Our embassy staff are discharging him from the hospital now.' Delphi felt a wave of relief course through her. Then Edward continued, 'I need you to pin this whole thing on the Russians.'

'But they haven't done anything.'

'Haven't they? You led me to believe Unity was innocent. Gabriel's dead. Jared said he got nothing from him anyway.'

'You think the whole thing's a set-up?'

'I think we're in a world of pain if we can't prove it is. This is slipping towards Armageddon quicker than the PM can announce the creation of a new independent inquiry.'

'Unity can still hear everything.'

'Unity, we need to talk. You do what you're best at: disappearing and uncovering what people don't want you to know. Then we'll sit down together and figure out where we go from there. You need protecting. That's something we can offer.'

'I don't need protecting.' Lior looked up and down the row of cars. There wasn't any movement.

'Money then? How much?'

'You can't afford it.' He pulled the door handle. 'I'm going.'

'Wait,' Delphi said, taking Lior's elbow and arresting his exit. 'I'll speak with him. Do we have leads on what we need from Vosinsk?'

'Ask our man,' came the reply. 'Find out what they're doing there. I'll send you details of the camp within the next half-hour.'

'Any contingency?'

'Either you find out who's behind the virus, who started this whole damn mess, or we're heading down an extremely dangerous path. I've bought you forty-eight hours. Then C's said the PM is stating Unity has evaded detection and I'm closing this down. We'll face the reaction and I can assure you, with things as they are, we're looking at moving to a complete breakdown of diplomatic relations.' Edward's voice dropped. 'And if you don't stay with us, Unity, I can't promise you our protection whether you think you need it or not.'

'The same protection you offered your wife and children?' Lior said.

There was silence. Delphi shot a glare of hatred at him.

Eventually, Edward replied. 'Bring him back alive would you, Delphi. As I say, I would like to talk to him.' He hung up.

'How did you – ? Why would you say that?'

'I don't trust him. It was a test; one he failed. Now let me go.'

'I'm coming with you.'

'Not this time.' He yanked his arm free and got out of the car.

'Afraid so,' she said, getting out of the passenger side calmly before walking around to meet him. He had knelt down beside a decades' old cream Lada 4x4 next to them and was removing a shoelace from a pair of brogues he had found behind his seat.

'Unless you want to meet the head of our cyber division tonight?'

Lior didn't answer. Instead he focused on tying a small loop in the middle of the lace. Then he pulled it down over the top of the Lada's driver window so that it dropped onto the door lock. He pulled the lock up and opened the door. Working quickly, he levered the steering column panel off with his multi-tool, connected the battery and ignition wires then sparked the starter. The engine roared into life and he turned to meet Delphi's cold state.

'You're quite capable, aren't you?'

'I don't need your help, if that's what you mean.'

'Don't test me,' she said.

He turned to sit down behind the wheel.

'A-uh, I'm driving,' Delphi said, taking his arm from the steering wheel and pushing it to his side. He resisted, stepping back to steady himself. She squared her face to his and looked him dead in his pupils.

'Don't.'

He glanced between her eyes – angry, unsure. Her powerful grip caused him to step back with his other foot, and he hesitated to use his full strength. He could feel the warmth of her buttery breath on his lips.

Then he relaxed his arm. She studied his face as it softened.

'Good decision,' she said, flicking a finger around to the passenger door. 'Now get in.'

Lior took his seat next to her and assumed a position so that his head was turned towards the window.

They left the city in silence and headed northeast along the E95 out of Kiev. They drove above affluent suburbs and then descended through industrial parks, until the warehouses and lorries were replaced by barns and tractors, then vast frosted fields – some ploughed, others sprouting leafy winter crops. They stretched out from the tarmac's edge like wings from a fragile butterfly; its dusted skin gleaming in the last of the pallid light.

Onwards lay the frozen tundra of Western Russia, and as they neared it an uncertain restlessness took over Lior; his mind would not be still. Inside, strange forces drew metals from his blood, and his stomach emptied, leaving him weak and agitated, jumping at the sight of pedestrians standing on the verge, waiting to cross the road with ghostly eyes fixed on his own. Sometimes he would see a spectre of himself in their place, and then it would disappear as the car's wheels hit cracks in the tarmac and his head left the window and then rattled back against it, grinding his cotton-dry teeth.

'I need to eat,' Lior eventually croaked, his seatbelt caught at his throat. So, after two hundred kilometres, Delphi guided the 4x4 into a Drava service station. The Russian border lay another one hundred kilometres ahead.

CHAPTER FIFTEEN

'Stay in the car,' Delphi said, looking over Lior's black, bloodstained trousers and combat jacket. 'We won't be able to get through border control. I'll get a map and some better clothing if they've got it. You can use the outside toilet when I get back. What size feet are you?'

'44.'

'What else do you want?'

'Lots of meat, and foil, aluminium foil.' He pushed his tongue to the roof of his mouth. 'Zinc, iron. Water.'

'Are you ill?'

He stared up at her with swollen, tormented eyes and said, 'Metal, I need metal.'

When Delphi returned, she handed Lior a shapeless pair of grey trousers the station had on special offer, a thick cream jumper and a black raincoat.

'These trousers are tasteless,' he said, but he put them on. Delphi let him change whilst she waited by the car. He knocked on the window when he was done.

'They didn't have any other boots,' Delphi said, getting in.

'It doesn't matter – these have held together for years.'

They drove onwards into the evening. Lior found a David Bowie collection in the car's audio system and they listened to *Rebel Rebel* and half of *The Man Who Sold the World* before Delphi switched to the radio. There were news reports about the escalations in the Arctic and the South-China Sea. This flowed into the hunt for the suspect behind the cyber-attack on Russia's military base and the bombing at Kiev Technical University, and how reports had been made suggesting a link between the two. Emergency video-conferences were taking place tonight between the British Prime Minister and Russian President.

Lior let his head lull back on the headrest, his eyes heavy. Strange how so much was being risked on proving his innocence. If the Russians had set the whole thing up then extraditing him would call their bluff, and they would play along; if they hadn't, then everything would be pinned on him regardless. Either way the growing tension would dissipate. Something more had to be going on.

He turned to follow Delphi's hands on the wheel. Then he traced the shape of her jacket's leather sleeve to her pale, soft neck.

'Stop watching me,' she said quickly. But Lior could sense a lack of conviction.

'Have you ever killed anyone?'

She didn't reply for a while, then, 'No.'

'It feels as though there's a disgust sitting in my stomach. A revulsion.'

'But you didn't do it.'

'I caused it. If I hadn't hacked Vosinsk, none of this would have happened.'

'I once asked my father to collect me from a friend's house rather than stay overnight as I had planned. It was January and late. The roads had frozen over. He wanted to wait until morning but I told him if he didn't I'd walk anyway. He lost traction on a corner and hit a lorry head on. Did I kill my father?'

Lior was quiet then. He wondered why Delphi would tell him something like that. She too had put a lot of faith in him. More than he imagined someone in her position would. He listened to her as she went on, trying to imagine her as an angst-ridden teenager who became consumed by grief and guilt, but single-minded enough to apply for MI6 anyway. Or be recruited.

'Most of the time I've managed to talk myself out of it – but there are times when I wonder what really separates me from someone driving whilst under the influence of alcohol, or deliberately not bothering to change the batteries in a smoke detector. Doing anything that endangers the lives of others knowingly to avoid a comparatively insignificant inconvenience. And these are people who have in return given up the rights and freedoms I have vowed to protect.'

'You were a child.'

'I was seventeen. How much can I have really changed in thirteen years? I'm the same person. I'm still capable of selfishness no matter how much I try to control it.'

'We can change. Our brains are plastic. If you're aware of your actions and have the will to change them, you can reshape who you are. But it starts with awareness, self-knowledge. The ability to observe yourself without bias. Which you have to an extent. Are we the same person years apart, anyway? Our cells are different, the atoms that make up our cells are different. What is the one constant that makes us who we are from one moment to the next? Information. Your mind. And your mind can be altered.'

Lior turned to face her.

'If scientists grew a comatose replica of your body in a tank from the moment of your birth, and then captured your brain state and copied it to this other body somehow. Rebuilt it cell by cell, dendrite by dendrite, and then in an instant, shut down your brain – whilst waking the other – you as you are now would cease to exist, but this other self would suddenly live, with memories up to the very moment before the procedure. Would you care that you were made of different atoms to your former self? Would you be the same person without the scar on your shin you got from learning to ride a bicycle?'

He let her think about it before adding, 'Each moment we are born again – only an illusion of self gives us a sense of being intransient.'

'And how pray is this illusion carried across to Atma? How is each cell or brain state, each connection mapped to a string of zeros and ones, and yet still *me*?'

'Well, if awareness is simply a representation of what we are attending to – if it is an informational model drawing on all the higher systems within our brain, including memories, other models such as our physiological, spatial and social systems, and of course our senses – producing a rich but inaccurate summary of what in each moment is most important and useful, then this information will be captured by Gabriel's total brain scan and upload. All that is needed is a connection and then learning software which uses the continuous signals from your central nervous system to emulate each infinitesimal element of the complete system. You have a simulation. But the information is the same.'

He looked away.

'That was the theory anyway. Gabriel always said that the quickest path to the singularity is through artificial super intelligence. But we do not yet entirely understand how to create a mind so the quickest thing to do is upload our own minds to machines.'

'You don't know that it works?'

Lior was silent.

'You don't know how it works, do you?' She looked at him. 'You really are just a foot soldier.'

Nothing.

'But he was your father,' she said, her voice softening. 'He didn't peel back the lid and take you through each step?'

'I just opened up supercomputers to expand the network so that it can hold enough people.'

'Or remnants of people.'

Lior watched a star on the horizon. It flickered in atmospheric dust. Then he said quietly, almost to himself, 'Perhaps remnants of him.'

His mind was quiet for a while before he thought of how every element in existence bar hydrogen and helium are themselves remnants of stars. We are stardust and children of the moment of creation.

They drove onwards in silence again for a while. Thinking.

Eventually, Delphi said, 'Something's obviously gone wrong, though – the program, the system, whatever you want to call it. Is it in you now? Is that what happened?'

'No. I was just finding storage for the system.'

He continued looking out of the window, bored with the same questions, frustrated he didn't have the answers. 'I told you that.'

'But you don't know what was going on behind the scenes. Perhaps it was already there. You're part of it now, it's in you and it can't get out. It's trying. It's spreading.'

'I know enough,' he snapped. 'Trust me.'

'Then you give me some hint as to why the hell your eyes have turned grey, your injuries have almost disappeared in a matter of hours, and you're speaking in tongues in your sleep.'

His fists tightened and he tried his best to control a rage building beneath his skin.

'I've told you, I don't know what has happened to me. Gabriel didn't know what happened to me. I need,' he breathed, 'to get to' – he did his best to not spit out the last word but it didn't help – 'Vosinsk.'

His arms were trembling now and Delphi stayed quiet. He just wanted to turn back the clock. He didn't want to be in a car with an MI6 officer about to enter Russia. He didn't want to be undergoing some kind of metamorphosis reminiscent of Franz Kafka and his travelling salesman. A strange presence growing within him. Whether this growth was physical or not, Lior couldn't tell.

His very bones seemed to be inhabited by a tingling sensation, sometimes it was painful. Like pins and needles. A burning. And then he was hardly aware of it at all. It came in waves. Or stages. Though perhaps it was all in his mind. But what an unhelpful phrase. Our minds are systems running on the hardware of our brains, our neurons. The information of our minds is as real, physically, as any other thing. As real as electricity.

Pine trees flashed past the window obscuring his view of the sky, bringing him back to the present. Delphi guided the car around a curve in the wide road sweeping through a forest. They could see only a hundred metres or so ahead, and being a few miles from the border, Lior could see the pads of Delphi's fingers turning white against the wheel. Lior stared at the ever-moving point where the road appeared from behind a dark mass of woodland. Something wasn't right.

Out of the gloom a police checkpoint shot into focus. Two police vans, an unmarked car, and red and white striped barriers startled Delphi into stomping the brake. Lior could see an officer checking the cab of an HGV whilst a dog was led around the vehicle. Delphi checked over her shoulder in preparation to turn around. But Lior knew that it was too late to turn back now. And even if the Ukrainians didn't currently have his profile, a quick vehicle check would reveal the Lada was stolen. Then they'd find gunshot residue on him and link DNA in specks of blood to Kiev. Soon enough everything would surface.

'Take the track on the right,' he said, 'and get ready to run.'

CHAPTER SIXTEEN

Delphi swung the wheel wildly and the 4x4 arced off the tarmac, landing on the gravelly dirt with a crunch. Before them, a dark bank of earth covered most of the entrance to a track leading down into the pine forest.

'Keep your speed,' Lior said.

The previously docile police officer checking the cab snapped his head around. 'Police, stop or I fire!' he shouted, drawing his firearm.

But Lior and Delphi had hit the bank. The Lada launched into the air, and there were seconds of nothing but the whine of engine revolutions and the hiss of wind against metal. The night sky filled the windshield, a half-moon hanging so close Lior thought he could reach out and touch it.

Then darkness swung back up from below.

The thump of the landing jolted their spines and shook them about like dice in a tumbler. The 4x4 smashed the underside of its bumper and chassis but continued to bounce down the dirt track.

'Head to the opening between the trees.'

'I can't see an opening,' Delphi shouted. 'I can't see a bloody thing.'

'Let me take it.' Lior reached over and held the wheel. 'Kill the lights.'

Lior kept the vehicle pointing down the path in the faint moonlight, bashing from one side of the bank to the other beneath the tall pines. It was getting steeper, and they were picking up speed. Then headlights flashed into the rear-view mirror, blinding them, and a corner came out of nowhere. Lior yanked the wheel.

They swept around a bend, rear wheels skidding out and crumbling the outer edge of the track, cascading dirt and rocks down into a torrential river. White-water spray covered glistening, ice-covered boulders and rose up above the banks so that the air was even cooler and crackling with ions. The deep roar of rapids rose above the whine of the engine.

At first they appeared to run parallel to the river, but it was soon obvious they were getting closer and closer to the water. And then, with twenty metres to go, the track turned into its icy depths. Delphi hit the brakes.

'Get out,' Lior told her.

'We can't outrun them. Not with dogs.' The UAZ 4x4 police vehicle behind them banked around the corner, its engine loud, headlights flashing with every bump like strobe lights. Barks and yelps muffled by the crashing of metal and cracking plastic.

'We'll cross the river,' Lior said.

'We'll freeze.'

'According to the sat-nav, there should be a village three miles on the other side of the border. If we move quickly we'll make it.'

They stood at the edge and looked for a stretch of water unbroken by boulders. The far bank could have been thirty metres away, but in the dark it was difficult to tell.

'Swim as fast as you can and don't stop.' Lior took her arm and pulled her into the torrent.

The bitter water hit him like a vice clamping around his chest. He tried to hold Delphi's wrist but she yanked it from him. She clawed furiously through the darkness and he did the same. Together they thrashed and kicked without pause, desperate to resist the current. It seemed to go on forever, their limbs burning. Lior tried to keep sight of Delphi as best he could in the swirls of shadowy water and raging spray thrown up from rapids and his wheeling arms.

Delphi hit land first, cracking her fingers against sharp rocks and gritty soil. Lior followed, scrambling up the wet, earthy embankment, ripping out thin roots with crooked fingers, trying to pull himself upwards, away from the agonising cold.

The ground dropped away without warning into darkness and he found himself spinning over a lip of tangled tree roots. He turned around, peering over them, back at the other side of the river. A figure crawled and stumbled beside him. He reached out and grabbed a limb – he figured it was her ankle. She thrashed as she did in the water whilst he felt for her mouth. He covered it and whispered harshly, 'Be quiet.'

She became still. 'Be quiet and wait,' he said. 'Let's see what they do.'

On the far bank they could make out silhouettes, both human and canine, pacing back and forth in front of the headlights. The lights pointed slightly upriver, and they had been dragged downstream, so it was likely they had not been seen coming ashore. Torch lights started shining onto the river closer to where they hid, flicking up and down as police officers meandered along searching for them in the water.

Lior and Delphi could only stand remaining still for thirty seconds or so before their bodies shook violently. 'Come on, otherwise we'll freeze. There should be a tributary not far from here that flows close to the village upstream.'

Lior half slid, half scrambled down over the lip of the

bank. Then he reached back to take Delphi's hand, and holding it, began to lead her through the forest until her eyes had adjusted to the darkness. They stomped over patches of brittle pine needles and through carpets of snow. The mighty roar of the river gave way to the calm and stillness of the forest floor, and the sweetness of pine and water swept into their lungs. After a while, the sound of a helicopter droned behind them in the distance for a few minutes, then faded away as it followed the river. Through breaks in the canopy high above, Lior tracked glimpses of the North Star. It led them into Russia.

They found a tributary. Running water forced the ice into patches for the first few metres. Further upstream it was completely frozen. Still, they could follow its serpentine shape beneath the snow. Twenty minutes later it veered west and they continued onwards in the direction they had been travelling, to the north, eyeing features on a mercurial horizon.

Shadows of rolling hills fell across wide, dark valleys – the glittering icicles and frosted fields punctured here and there by silhouettes of lonely oaks and ruined farmhouses. Above them were cast a thousand stars and the still rising moon.

They came across no roads, no sign of recent human life. Lior said the village should be over the next horizon line but one, and he continued onwards without rest.

At first Delphi fought to regain any lost ground moments after losing it, but bit-by-bit the gap between them widened. No matter how much reserve she drew upon, her legs tired and ached with the cold. Now she followed what looked like his footsteps across the dark expanse – saw how they disappeared beneath a copse of trees. She grunted and forced herself onwards, desperate to make it there before Lior reached another spot that concealed him from view.

At the copse the ground became a plateau and provided some respite. Stumbling over slippery, fallen trees, cracking branches beneath her boots, she made it to the open ground on the other side. Lior was halfway across another vast field, a shrinking phantom in a sea of murky white and tufts of grass.

Cupping her mouth with her hand, she called his name. But he didn't turn. She called again.

Lior first caught a glimpse of light when they were halfway across the valley floor. It was soft and yellow, perhaps a window lit by a shaded lamp. His pace quickened.

Continuing onwards, he skirted along the frayed edge of the pine forest until, from atop the crest of a rolling gulley, he could see a weathered stone farmhouse tucked away just inside the trees. A ribbon of wood smoke drifted upwards from a slanted chimney. Below, long unused stables and courtyards jutted out from the central homestead, built on in years gone by when life was good. Now it appeared to be almost non-existent. He turned one hundred metres or so from the house, waiting for Delphi to catch up. She eventually staggered into view with a worsening limp.

'Thanks for waiting for me,' she said, her voice laced with breathy sarcasm.

'It's best we approach together,' Lior replied, eyeing the house. He could make out a blurred figure standing downstairs at a smoky, paned window. He strode towards it.

Drawing closer, the figure disappeared. Then the front door opened revealing a withered man in layers of thick jumpers with wispy hair. A shotgun hung open over his forearm. The other hand held a cartridge. He stared at them motionless with large, glassy eyes.

'Zdravstvuyte,' *hello,* Lior called out in Russian.

The man's voice was croaky, as if unused for a long time, but it grew in strength. 'What business have you in my valley?'

'I didn't know this was your valley.' They continued walking.

'Where are you from?' the man snapped.

'We're just travellers. We came for a walking holiday but are lost and tired. Can we stop for a while to rest and dry our feet? Perhaps you will be able to direct us to the nearest town.'

'You must be very lost, yes? And simple minded to be walking at night at this time of year. There is nothing for many miles.'

'Except you it seems?'

'This is my home.'

'I am from Kiev, my father was a professor at the university. My mother was from Donetsk.'

'I hope they had more sense than you.'

He eyed them for a few moments, and then seemed to decide that they'd spoken enough. 'You may rest for a short time, and dry your clothes. But if you're not who you say you are, I'll feed you to my pigs.'

He turned and walked back inside, leaving the door ajar.

CHAPTER SEVENTEEN

Lior and Delphi placed their boots in front of the hissing fire and hung their wet socks over the back of an adjacent chair. The man sat down in an armchair across from them, placed his shotgun against the wall behind him, then rekindled his pipe. He glanced up. 'If you stand either side of the fire your clothes should dry.'

They exchanged glances.

'Could we help ourselves to a glass of water?' Lior said.

The old man looked to the kitchen area, back towards the door. It consisted of a wood-fuelled stove, a stone basin and a mix of cabinets from the middle of the last century, some older. Jars and bottles filled with pickles, grains and other indiscernible substances dotted the worktops and homemade shelves.

'The pipe to the spring has frozen,' he said, looking back to the fire, 'but there is a bucket from the well beneath the sink.'

Lior walked over and took two glasses from an open shelf above a window that looked out to the snowfields beyond. As he bent down he thought he glimpsed a horse passing between a line of trees in the distance, but he could not be certain. He dipped the glasses into the bucket and waited for some sediment to settle before presenting one to Delphi.

'There isn't much to eat,' the old man said, still staring at

111

the fire.

So they stood in silence and sipped the ice-cold water gingerly whilst studying what they could see of the house. The main room – with the basic kitchen, farmhouse dining table and 1960s-style, patched-up, tan armchairs in front of the fire – was modest. Hanging from the beams were blackened pots and pans and some dried herbs. Rosemary, tarragon, dill.

Rising from the far end of the worn terracotta-tiled floor stood freestanding bookshelves stuffed with reference, history and poetry works, and more jars, trinkets and a number of yellowing postcards. The house smelt of wood smoke, musty paper, wet leaves and just a hint of lavender from a bar of hand soap on the windowsill above the basin.

Lior's eyes came to rest on the two armchairs in front of him, one chair cupping the withered man puffing away on a glowing pipe. Beside him, on a low table between the chairs, sat a chessboard halfway through a game. Lior realised that if it was the black's turn, black could force a checkmate by sacrificing its central knight then moving the queen to g4 and the one remaining bishop to a5 on the subsequent turn.

Lior gestured with his glass towards the board. 'Are you playing against yourself?'

The man continued drawing on his pipe, but looked up to eye Lior. 'No, of course not.' He breathed out small wisps of smoke from the corners of his mouth and nostrils then lit a match to resurrect the dying fire in the bowl of his pipe. 'I can't stand the game,' he said out of the corner of his mouth, then flicked his glance up towards the door. 'My wife wins every time.'

The door to the house slammed inwards, caught by a gust of icy, snow-filled air, and cracked against the stonework. A woman in a sheepskin coat and leather boots stepped inside.

She had a large plastic shopping bag in one hand, a small messy-haired mongrel dog under that arm and a bundle of logs under the other.

'Gregor,' she shouted, turning to kick the door closed behind her. 'Put the damn samovar on.'

She dropped the mongrel and logs to the floor and took a few steps towards the kitchen, then stopped and looked over towards the fire. She glanced at Gregor then back at Lior and Delphi.

'Oh … hello. We were not expecting visitors.' She stood motionless, her reddish curled hair just visible beneath a patterned scarf tied over her head. She had a pretty face, high cheeks and bright eyes. The years had been kind to her.

'No,' Lior replied. 'We were walking and became lost. Your husband generously let us warm ourselves by the fire.'

'Just passing through then, I see.' She studied them for a few moments longer, then abruptly continued into the kitchen area and busied herself with the bag of shopping.

'Well, that's alright, because I have only picked up enough vodka to see Gregor and me through the week.'

She stood a litre bottle on the kitchen worktop then pulled out a folded newspaper from the bag. 'I can always send him out again once you're on your way.'

She stopped and looked at them.

'But what am I saying? It is late and you both look exhausted and soaked to the bone. We better get something hot inside you and find some dry clothes.' She walked around the wooden worktop separating off the kitchen and inspected them with greater thoroughness.

'Gregor, why have you let our guests stand here catching their death?' She turned and clipped him over the back of his head with the crisp newspaper. He flinched, clutching his pipe, then got to his feet grumbling.

'He's useless in the evening unless he's had a drink. Then he soon perks up a bit. Start putting things away, will you. Come along, my darlings. Let's get you out of these clothes.'

And so Lior and Delphi followed her up stone steps, revealed behind a heavy curtain and knotted door beside the kitchen.

After much good-hearted fussing and various clothes being held up to their frames by Marta, as they came to learn her name, they reappeared downstairs in thick jumpers, corduroys and woollen slippers.

Marta had not been flippant about Gregor. They found him with a glass of vodka, dancing over to a lit polished-brass samovar, which stood proudly on the dining table like some kind of shrine. He had a swaying shuffle that lagged slightly behind the Tatar-like accordion rhythms emanating from a radio on the kitchen windowsill. He stopped and his beaming smile and moist eyes looked up to framed black-and-white portrait photographs on the wall behind the table. Marta stepped into the room behind them as he started filling a teapot with steaming water from the ornate samovar. He glanced over.

'Tea? Or something stronger?'

And so they spent the rest of the night in candlelight, drinking smoky Keemun tea, then sampling a variety of pickled vegetables with black bread and cold meats, washed down with plenty of vodka kept cool in a bucket of snow beneath the table.

The fire spat beside them and Marta, with occasional interjections from Gregor – largely out of self-defence – told

Lior and Delphi about how life had changed for them over the decades. How they had grown up locally then studied in St Petersburg before travelling through the Americas for a number of years.

They had loved Cuba and ended up running a bar in Havana whilst saving money to continue travelling south. Gregor had resumed his studies then worked as an engineer when they returned. Marta played violin in an orchestra and toured for a while. But they longed to get out of the city, to slow down, enjoy the seasons, and eventually to return to the fields, woods and rivers of their childhoods. Soon after, Gregor inherited the farm.

They had largely lived off the land ever since. Times had been good. Friends and relatives were plentiful. But the seasons went by. Friends died. Relatives moved away or started families and had less time to share with others. Work dried up as it did everywhere, and the cost of living continued to climb.

'But enough of this lament,' Marta suddenly exclaimed. 'Tell us of your own lives.'

Delphi looked at Lior.

'Well,' he said. 'We live in London,' he looked to Delphi, then back at Marta, stretching out the silence. 'I'm studying.'

Marta gestured for him to elaborate.

'If I'm not on my computer I spend a lot of time … in libraries, or just wandering around parks.' He looked at Delphi again. 'Thinking.'

Marta turned to Delphi. 'Is he always so spiritless? How do you put up with it?'

Delphi smiled. 'I don't really. I tend to do my own thing.' So then Delphi skimmed over a semi-autobiographical account of where she had grown up and what she did to fill

115

her days.

'You two are both as secretive as spies,' Marta said. 'You must have been made for each other.' Delphi smiled, her bucked incisor caught over her bottom lip, and glanced at Lior. He had raised his eyebrows in admonishment.

'They've talked enough,' Gregor said, getting to his feet. 'What is there to know of life? It goes on.'

Then he looked up, as if in a trance, his hands cupped together by the side of his head. 'It is time,' he looked down at them, 'to dance.' And he clapped out a resounding ta-ta-ta-tat, ta-ta-ta-tat, ta-ta-ta-tat over and over and looked at Marta and flicked his head towards the next room.

'Oh, go on then,' she said. 'You've persuaded me.' And she dragged herself up from the wooden bench and disappeared in the darkness behind a moss green curtain covering a door, into what she had earlier called the music room.

Delphi and Lior caught each other's eyes. They were both bemused but smiled sweetly when the mournful strident sound of a single string vibrating beneath a bow filled the space around them.

Marta reappeared, still drawing the horsetail across her violin. Gregor continued clapping. Marta bent low, a pain carried within the sound doubling her over. As the deep, full note came to a close, she let it disperse into the night, waiting for every trace of it in the air and stone to settle.

Then swiftly she stood again, her back arched as if to show off her heart, and an arpeggio of notes flew from the body of the instrument in a flurry of gypsy influenced melodies from centuries past.

Gregor leapt into the air, still clapping. On landing, he stamped his foot against the ground as if it were a drum.

Marta weaved around him, her yellow skirt flung out like a spinning tutu. The fire roared behind, sending dancing shadows across the stone walls and beamed ceiling. Lior topped their glasses with vodka then sat back with Delphi to drink in the spectacle. They were not quite in the mood for taking part given the circumstances, but to watch, and listen, was a thing they would not have changed for the world.

Later, when the candles had burned low, the firewood within the house had gone and Delphi had coaxed a family recipe for Olivier salad out of Marta, Gregor cleared away the dishes to the kitchen. He was listening to a crackly late night broadcast on a radio, a play, a re-run of afternoon programming. He laughed throatily on occasion and once clapped his hands together, joy in the corners of his eyes.

Marta had gone upstairs to prepare herself for bed. She returned as Gregor was finishing up and made a nest for Lior and Delphi in the music room, where it was warm beside the wall with the fire.

As Gregor and Marta were about to make their way upstairs, Lior asked them how he and Delphi could get to the nearest town.

'If there was not so much snow I would take you,' said Gregor. 'And I'm afraid we only have one horse. But there is a track, for the loggers inside the wood, not far. If you go north, you'll come to a train line. There is also a road not much further along. This road takes you to the town. There you can take a bus. Or stay there. Whatever you want. But I'll point the way in the morning. After breakfast.' He slapped a surprisingly firm hand on Lior's shoulder.

They said their goodnights, then – when they were alone

– Delphi and Lior looked at each other in wonder. Delphi glanced away first and went about gathering her things.

'We should move our clothes closer to the fire,' Lior said, breaking the silence. 'Be ready to move at first light.'

Delphi was approaching the doorway to the music room and looked back. 'I'm not sleeping in the same bed as you, obviously. You can sleep by the fire. I'll pass you a few cushions.'

'It's not like you're a married woman.'

'You are continually full of assumptions.'

Lior observed her. 'It's Jared isn't it?'

She stopped in the middle of the doorway, her back to him. Then she turned and said, 'Don't ever assume anything about me. You don't know anything about my life. No one does.'

She went through to the music room and Lior could hear her carefully opening the drawers and then cupboards beneath an underpowered bulb. He stooped to stoke the fire, carefully concentrating the embers together beneath the remaining wood.

They could still be going through a divorce, Lior thought. Or perhaps they had never officially tied the knot. He had to hand it to her: her digital profile was watertight. He couldn't be certain what he knew about her anymore. What were truths, what were lies. But what he did know is that a woman like her shouldn't have to end up with a man as aggressive and obnoxious as Jared.

Perhaps only in a world where few others could ever know the ins and outs of her life, and what lay beneath her façade. We are both so alone, he thought, gazing through a gap in the thick curtains, at what he thought was the same solitary star he had seen from the road earlier.

After a few minutes Delphi whispered back to him harshly, 'This was a stupid idea. I could be halfway to Vosinsk by now. We have no transport, our clothes are ruined, my hip was smashed against a rock in the river.' She came through with an old-fashioned nightgown draped over one arm. 'And we appear to have arrived back in the eighteenth century. We'll have to make up time tomorrow, once we've had some sleep.'

She covers over her vulnerability with pragmatism, Lior thought.

The radio crackled.

'Not quite the eighteenth century.' Lior said. He touched the radio to attempt to tune it, but a triumphant orchestral tune immediately sounded, though it was so distorted Lior had to hold the tinny speaker to his ear. The music cut to electronic beeps before an elegant voice began reporting the news at midnight.

Lior mouthed words silently, his eyes searching the embers for the translations. Then he spoke aloud, 'United in … condemnation of Europe's cover-up of … a deliberate probing attack on Russia, China and Russia have … decided to act bilaterally … in closing the Northeast Passage and trade routes through the South China Sea. They are also stepping up joint naval exercises off the south coast of Japan and drilling operations within the Arctic … the United States has reacted angrily to further foot-dragging by the UK government …'

The signal died for a few seconds, then Lior listened again and said, 'In a separate move the United Islamic Caliphate has … cut off oil exports to Europe following further strikes against one of its training facilities … in the north of the region and continued support to rebel forces.

119

With unconfirmed reports of a skirmish between Chinese and Japanese forces … just north of the Senkaku Islands taking place a few hours ago … many international observers are calling for calm in what …'

The voice broke up completely, leaving Lior and Delphi listening to static, perhaps from the chaos that generated fractal snowflakes hanging above them now as heavy clouds rolled over the valley. Undoubtedly from background microwave radiation, which filtered through the cosmos as an eternal reminder of the impermanence of existence: what begins must end.

Lior leant a straightened arm against the large mantelpiece over the smouldering fire. He spoke first.

'When we get to Vosinsk, we will find out the truth and then tell the world.'

'Something tells me that the world doesn't want to hear the truth.' Delphi folded the gown in front of her and held it to her chest.

'In that case, let's hope it's an act of revolution.'

'Against who?'

'I have a feeling the truth of what has happened in the last few days goes beyond our comprehension of revolution as we know it. I just hope I am not its casualty.'

Delphi unexpectedly reached out and held Lior's upper-arm. 'I'm as driven to get to the bottom of this as you are, Lior. And whatever happens at Vosinsk, we'll get you back to the UK. We'll look after you.'

'Your future is not either being obliterated by a computer program or being sent to a work camp in Siberia.'

Delphi dropped her arm.

'Lior, I'm a member of the UK's Secret Intelligence Service in a hostile power, you don't have any idea of what

I'm risking here do you?'

He was silent.

'As ever, you are oblivious to everything going on in those around you. I'd say goodnight but you wouldn't notice if I left. Oh, and don't think about running, I'll track you in the snow and have no qualms about using force if you don't stop. Lethal or otherwise.'

She turned and swept across the rough tiled floor to the doorway, slipping through into the darkness of the side room, leaving Lior with nothing to do but turn and stare at the greying embers cradled by an iron grate. A lone figure in a shadowy and silent house.

A Chinese and Japanese conflict. China and Russia opposing Europe and the United States. He'd heard in Kiev of Pakistan moving to support China. India as ever was behind the West. He had not caused all of this. But where tensions had been smouldering, an attack on one side by the other had ignited them. He had jeopardised everything. Not only eternity but the present as well.

CHAPTER EIGHTEEN

Lior left at dawn, before anything else in the house had stirred. He had dressed quietly in the dark, listening to the rise and fall of Delphi's breath from the pitch black depths, wondering whether she would wake from her dreams, and if not, whether he would see her again. He hoped he might, though in another time, another place. Perhaps another world. He wanted to stay and wake with her, but this was a journey he had to make alone. It was true, he hadn't really thought of the danger she herself was in, and the threat to her life would only grow as they entered Russia, he by her side.

He entered the wood whilst the sky to the east became a pale blue, like thawing water on a puddle of black ice caught in the glowing sun. A dark withered canopy hung above him, powdered snow floating down in an eternal blanket, settling on his eyelashes and inside his collar, down the back of his neck where his skin blushed and stung with the bitterness of it. His hair became white as he drew his coat about him and trudged onwards, deep into the endless forest of needle-like trees, dark spindly branches cradling slithers of snow against a bluish mist that enveloped the wood.

He came across the track, a corridor through trunks with snapped-off branches sweeping north, parallel dips in the snow over deep ruts disappearing to a point around a distant curve, where more trees stood tall like sentinels. He marched onwards, sodden boots stinging frozen feet, his trousers slowly saturating from the shins up until they rubbed between his already raw thighs like wire wool. His breath was rasping and throat sore.

At the bend in the track, Lior stopped to listen and look back. Where he had come from was now lost amid the trees: even his footsteps were slowly vanishing forever. Delphi had not followed him and soon his tracks would be gone.

He turned to continue walking, looking up as he took a first step, but in the distance, at the next bend, stood a wolf.

Its eyes were steady on Lior. Its breath condensing in two jets from glistening nostrils. It was a stunning sight. Lior felt a calmness descend over his mind whilst his heart began to thump against the inside of his chest. The beauty of the moment took hold of him, facing each other, now in this place, whilst the endless forest engulfed them, Lior felt as though he had been led here.

The wolf was who he had come to witness. He who lived in the wild, rejecting man, unlike his ancestors before him. This animal stood proud, alone, self-sufficient if necessary. Unmoved by Lior. And yet, Lior could sense, or could project onto it, a feeling of respect; not fear, nor ambivalence, nor hatred. They stood for the longest time.

At first, Lior filed through the standard responses to being confronted by wild animals, and wolves in particular. It should back away if I speak, or else I should backtrack. If it follows, appear as large and loud as possible. Some part of him felt as though he should confront it. Perhaps if he were a real man he would not back down from his intention to pass.

In combination, his adrenaline and testosterone could drive him to fight. If necessary to strike and kick. He could test his will to survive, to place his wits against another animal of similar size, to face death and struggle with grit and blood against it.

But as the wolf turned to look over its shoulder, and then back at Lior, his awareness reached out to the wolf, its eyes again fixed on his. His awareness modelled his own attention, but it also modelled the attention of others. It bestowed on those who could be assumed to possess intention, an awareness: other individuals – so that we may see the world through their eyes; and in earlier times, as a derivative, the wind, and sea and sun; perhaps even the universe itself.

The wolf was a social animal, Lior knew. It was useful for it to be able to predict the actions of not only others but of itself in relation to others. It too projected some form of awareness onto Lior. More basic yes, through the eyes of a wolf, Lior was a mystery, but he was still an animal. Lior was tall, slender – perhaps a threat, perhaps prey. No judgement had yet risen up victorious in its similarly probabilistic and hierarchically predictive mind, out-competing the other.

Lior felt his awareness connect with that of the wolf's, meeting it somewhere in space, or outside of space. And there was a stillness. True mindfulness, not forced attention; lower functions could be left to deal with the senses. A quiet mind in which only awareness remained. The model of the attention system only attending to the model of the attention system. Awareness observing itself in an introspective cyclical loop of unending depths.

Lior and the wolf together seemed to sink deeper and deeper into a hall of mirrors. And with this they transcended time. The falling snow about them stopped mid-flight, and hung suspended in air that had previously whistled around a spinning planet that chased a star shooting around the centre of a galaxy, which in turn swept towards an inevitable impact with another, inside space that itself was accelerating apart.

What space *is* was unknown to Lior at that time. As was its precise relationship with time; if there were ultimately a difference between the two. But he felt as though in that moment he at least knew the nature of both and could rise beyond either.

The smell of sweat and some blood reached the wolf's awareness, rising up through its brain, a snowball triggering an avalanche, and the wolf lowered its head and raised a front paw to advance.

At that moment, Lior's reflexes began a parallel search for a response to the wolf's approach.

In a heartbeat he had begun to sing. The sound of his voice breaking the quiet, surprising his conscious self, as if it were not him. But it was – it was a part of him he did not know still existed. Memories locked away, now found by a system within him capable of perfect recall. He sang a sweet song that his mother had sung to him on the day of her visit. She had calmed him with its ebb and flow of low folk melody. He had a deep voice that resonated within his chest and lifted up with the tallest of the pines around him.

Oh, there on the mountain
Oh, there on the steep one
Oh, there were sitting a couple of doves
They were sitting and mating
Embracing with their bluish wings
The hunter appeared from behind the steep mountains
He broke, he tore apart this couple of doves

The wolf stopped stalking towards Lior and listened intently.

He killed the male dove and caught the female
He brought her home and put her on the floor

Sitting down on his hinds in the snow, the wolf looked up as a woodpigeon flew over Lior, towards it, and then continued on along the path. The wolf remained looking upwards, beyond the canopy and to the sky. As Lior continued singing, it let out a long wailing howl that reverberated out into the depths of the wood around them, and into the hills beyond.

My dove, bluish-winged,
Why are you so sad?
I have seven pairs of doves
Fly and choose. Maybe there is one for you?
I've already flown and I tried to choose
But none of them are the one I lost

Lior brought the final note to a rounded close and let the hush descend over them once more. The only sound was a creaking branch above them and the distant echoes of other wolves replying to their kin. If the wild had a sound, then Lior could in that moment hear it on the wind.

The wolf was still for a while, then looked back at Lior and lowered its head, seemingly in an act of obeisance – although it could have been to re-consider Lior's scent. Lior dared to hope the former and responded in kind, dipping his head with equal poise. Neither averted their eyes. Then the wolf turned and trotted away, around the corner and out of sight, leading a path through the trees. Disappearing back into the wilderness.

Upon finally leaving the edge of the forest, Lior came across the railway line in a flat, rural expanse of uncultivated land, where grasses stuck up above the carpet of snow. Withered hornbeam birches dotted the landscape and the horizon was absent in ghostly veils of mist sweeping across the endless fields.

After many miles, Lior heard a rolling tremor behind him, and he moved quickly until he had reached a curve in the tracks around a bend in a frozen river. Waiting behind a snowdrift, he let the train slow before the bend and then come level.

It was solely freight, carrying what looked like coal, ore, stacks of timber and some chemical or perhaps radioactive cargo. Freight cars bolted and shrieked by in a scream of steel on steel and roaring diesel. Sighting what he had hoped for, he clawed at the snow, scrambling to his feet, and then he charged across the grassy slush. Bounding like a foal in his final steps, beside sealed tanks adorned in hazard symbols, he leapt.

An empty flat-bed carriage tore into the space beneath him, and – clipping his shoulder and hip – spun him violently down its length, wearing through one arm of his raincoat before spitting him off its rear as quickly as he had landed.

His stomach hit a coupler, knocking the breath from his lungs and swinging his shins into the tubular buffers beneath him. His hands clung to the underside of the greased frozen steel, and he waited for the sudden excruciation to ease whilst grit flashed past his face a few feet below.

With considerable effort he shuffled along the coupler back towards the end of the flatbed carriage. Taking hold of the riveted edge, he hauled himself up, and kicking wildly, rolled over onto the dimpled metal sheeting.

Lying on his back, his clothing wet and torn, his skin blistered, ripped and bloodied, fingers stinging, and struggling for breath, Lior watched insipid low clouds glide past overheard, shrouding a bleached sky. Hypnotised by moving rhythmically through an unearthly cocoon that he was unable to focus his vision on, whilst raw agony rushed adrenaline through his veins, he strangely felt more alive than he could ever remember. If a few hours earlier he was pure consciousness, this was the cold hard reality of the physical world.

He lay further along the carriage floor for much of the journey, better to stay low in order to avoid being seen. He was in the lea of the next freight car, partially sheltered from the chilled wind fighting to get through every gap in his clothing. The pain had subsided, probably with numbness, although looking at his hands now the torn skin on his knuckles had seemed to knit together in just the two or three hours since it had split open. He rested his limbs back on the dimpled metal, a hastily made tourniquet keeping his right upper arm from falling apart. All being well, it wouldn't be long before all of this made sense.

His fingers came to rest on what felt like grit. He scooped a little of it in a fist and brought it to his face. Jagged, dark crushed stone that caught the ashen light. Tasted like metal. He ate some more. It nourished what grew within him.

CHAPTER NINETEEN

After many hours, Lior was awoken by a jolt. He pushed himself to sitting, legs still outstretched. The train had come to a halt among a series of low warehouses and rail-track exchanges. The walls of the buildings were corrugated metal, the rooftops hidden beneath thick blankets of snow. Grit and gravel mixed with slush lined the rails and criss-crossing paths to outbuildings and cranes. Everywhere else was white, even the pines, standing tall around the compound like the walls of a fortress. He could taste salt in the air.

Astonishingly his wounds had healed a great deal, although the deepest cuts had turned dark and almost metallic. He couldn't feel anything but fear at what was happening to him, but he was powerless to stop it. He needed to reach Vosinsk. He needed answers.

Two men in heavy fluorescent jackets and hard hats – one broad-shouldered, the other slight – crossed a set of tracks towards the front of the train. One of them did the motion of slicing your neck open to the locomotive at the front, undoubtedly the driver.

The engine died.

Lior quickly dropped down between the carriages onto the sleepers, on the far side of the coupling so that he was hidden. His legs felt sprightly and he landed with little sound.

The men reached the front of train and Lior could hear gruff voices and the stamping of feet for a few seconds. He craned his head around the container behind him. The smaller man was walking towards him down the train, checking the load and coupling. Just as he turned from checking the fourth freight car, Lior pulled himself back away from the edge, out of view. His heart quickened and he watched as a great billow of his breath condensing in the icy air rose out from the side of the train.

He needed to move.

He slipped beneath the coupling and checked the other side of the freight car. With his back against it, he looked over to where the men had come from, at the closest building to the train, a pre-fabricated shack at the end of a line of storage and lorry depots. The type of building which springs up on a worksite. Normally containing a collapsible laminate top table on a lino floor, and a stained kettle and packet of biscuits in the corner. This one had caged windows with mottled green walls and steel mesh steps up to a flimsy door. Next it to sat two vehicles: a large white transit van and a navy SUV.

Lior smiled.

Slipping into the site office, the first thing that hit Lior was a giant map of Western Russia on the far wall; the rest of the room was almost as he imagined it, even replete with an old gas fire that stank of burnt dust. He padded up to the map. It was held together with plastic tape and dotted with pen marks and scribbles. The train lines had been traced with a red marker, and he followed a central one down through Moscow to the Ukrainian border. Back at the top it ended at a place called Severodvinsk, just west of Arkhangelskoye, where the Dvina River flows into the White Sea and onwards into the Arctic. He remembered from studying the Soviet economy at school in Kiev that Severodvinsk is home to the world's largest shipyard. Built to service the Northern Fleet and load submarine-launched ballistic missiles. Now undoubtedly key in helping Russia dominate its resource-rich northern coast and yesterday in closing the Northeast Passage to the West.

He recalled Delphi's map of Vosinsk he had studied in the car and placed it twenty miles east along the coast from there. Perhaps this was why Russia had squared-off to the UK so determinedly following his hack: it was a little close for comfort. But then again, who knew what lay at Vosinsk, somewhere not even shown on public maps? He took a mental image of the one before him and – stuffing the half-eaten packet of biscuits into his jacket pocket – looked around for a set of keys.

No keys. But he did find a Gazprom workman uniform in a locker. It was a blue boiler suit, logo on the back, and an ID card of one Oleg Kozlov clipped to its top left pocket. He folded it over one arm.

Looking through a mucky window he studied the white van outside. It had panels instead of rear side windows, and the distinctive, blue flame logo of Gazprom slapped on the side. He slipped out of the office and crunched through compacted snow to the driver's side and looked down at the dashboard. There was just an on button to the left of the steering wheel. No ignition and no keys.

He glanced over the bonnet back towards the train. Saw the inspecting worker had reached the end and was now walking back down the near side of the freight cars.

Lior ducked back behind the van and tried the driver's door. It wouldn't open. There was no keyhole and no catch for the window, unlike the ancient Lada. But he did feel a slit inside the handle. He slipped the ID card on the uniform up into the handle and the car unlocked with a satisfying, soft clunk. Employees use only – he supposed it stopped the problem of losing the keys. He carefully swung open the door, climbed inside, and drew it back to the van without closing it fully.

He sat back in the chair, head taut against the headrest to minimise his profile. A crash and clang of metal on metal and then a rolling echo rung out to his right. He looked to the train and watched as the three men peered into the first carriage, the side of it now open.

The thumb of his left hand, previously resting on the ignition button, punched forward, depressing it. The car's electric motor whirred to life, generating an artificial warning purr. He began to roll forward so gently that the pines beside him could have instead swayed in the wind. With a slight turn, he listed towards a track heading between the trees, dark ruts clear of snow. He watched the men clamber again into the freight train in the rear-view mirror. One of them broke into a box to check its contents. Opportunistic skimmers of freight, Lior decided. He wasn't sure whether to wish them luck or not. In the scheme of things, what they found or didn't on the train that day mattered little. Life, he decided, could be seen as a series of small victories or defeats; one person's triumph, of course, being another's despair, and who was he to decide right and wrong? And what connection does right or wrong have with victory or defeat anyway? Neither have any immutability: each welter on an open, anthropic sea.

The men grew smaller until they disappeared behind the slowly steepening decline, and Lior merely let gravity carry him away from a wearying journey, like the tide carries flotsam. His destination was only thirty minutes or so by road. His small victory today in the great scheme of things, for good or for worse.

CHAPTER TWENTY

Lior pulled off the road one hundred metres before the only sign to Vosinsk, set in front of a turning off to the right in a barren wilderness. He could just see a skeletal radio dish rising above pine trees in the distance. Before them lay open ground carpeted with old muddied snow. The road up to the camp was the same grey and weathered tarmac – seemingly bleached beneath blinding Arctic sunlight. A couple of red bollards were strewn haphazardly across it a few metres up from the turning.

Lior stepped out of the vehicle. The brittle icy grass crunched beneath his boots. He stretched his arms and shook cramp from his legs. He took a deep breath of the crisp, saline air. Felt its chill about his temples and his eyes prick with tears as the inhalation turned into a yawn. It had been a long journey, but he was here now and a tension rose in him silently with a furious intensity, until he was left hollow and sick to the stomach.

He had to pull himself together. He stomped his feet to drive heat into his legs. Rubbed his hands. Watched the distant pines. He had changed into the Gazprom boiler suit – ID on his left breast pocket – and run his split and dirty fingers through his hair until it was presentable, if not smart.

Using a pair of binoculars he had found in the glove box of the van, Lior leant over the bonnet and eyed what he could of the camp through the trees. The gate looked to be guarded by one individual, armed, with undoubtedly at least one other in the pillbox next to him. With the aid of the binoculars and improved vision, he could read the serial number on the side of the AK-12 rifle hundreds of metres away. He could see cameras rising up from the wire fence, as he had expected, with a roll of barbed wire between them. Having contemplated trying to break his way into the installation, he now felt he had confirmed the wisdom of a less risky approach. Being denied access due to a lack of sufficient ID was preferable to getting caught whilst cutting through a wire fence in the dead of night by a junior soldier carrying an assault rifle.

He got back into the van.

Trundling towards the line of trees, he took in the entrance beyond them. It was just as he remembered from the news report. The road snaked towards the main gate, a lowered red barrier jutting out from a squat brick building. A soldier was leaning into an open window of the guardroom with his rifle hanging loosely at his side, his back to the approach. Lior slowed as he drew close, lowered his driver window and held the ID card with his forefinger partially obscuring the photo. The soldier glanced over at the vehicle, spotted the logo on the side panelling, and said, 'Where is your vehicle pass?'

Lior didn't blink. 'I left it back in the main office. What's happening on the news?' He indicated to the display screen the soldier had been watching in the guardroom. Another man in a luminescent yellow security coat sat inside with his eyes glued to the shaky images of a lush ridgeline dotted with rickety farmhouses. Panicking men, women and children, who looked to be from the Indian sub-continent, ran past the camera, rushing to flee some unspoken devastation that lay beyond the temporary safety of their valley. Judging by the red eyes, coughing and saliva, Lior guessed that a chemical attack had occurred on the Pakistani-Indian border. Terrorist or otherwise.

'Pakistan has attacked India,' the soldier said. 'Don't know why.' He stepped to the end of the barrier and raised it whilst watching the images. Lior toed the accelerator, his heart racing.

'Make sure you bring your vehicle pass next time. I get more spot checks now since the cyber-attack.'

'I will. Thank you,' said Lior. And as he edged onto the camp without hindrance he watched the soldier, first with the corner of his eye, and then in his side mirror. He didn't move again from the window.

Not much changes, Lior thought. The security of a small army camp was much the same as when he'd undergone national service. The guards underpaid and unperturbed. Once at his first unit they'd even let an old face come and go without checking his ID for almost a year after he'd been discharged. That's just the way it was. Contractors came and went. And who cared when an atrocity could tip two nations with nuclear weapons into war? If he'd been on guard duty, nine times out of ten he wouldn't either.

Lior turned right, following a sign to the research department. Before him were perhaps two football pitches of large, old hangers, most of which looked derelict. Open snowy expanses lay between them and he could see two lit windows ahead. The long Arctic night was drawing in so that the sky was now a dark, sea lion grey, and the snow turned sallow beneath the illuminated windows.

Above all of this, rising out of the roof of a block-like building, standing like a great gaping skeletal eye, dwarfing the

135

other structures beneath it, a monolith, a colossal radio dish from the Cold War – angled at the heavens. It seemed to grow as Lior drove steadily towards its base, for it rose higher and higher into the darkening sky as he met the offices beneath it, until the roof of the van hid its pinnacle from view. One of the lit windows he had seen was an office in the far corner of the ground floor.

Lior pulled up in an empty parking bay by the main door, next to the only other car outside the building, and switched off the engine. He listened to the pin-drop silence within which nothing around him moved, and then let out a long, slow breath. He got out and walked to the door. It was locked but the only numbers not frozen over on a keypad to one side of it were 1459. It took him five attempts to gain entry on 9415. Inside, he headed to the far corner, down a grey linoleum corridor, passing windows into open plan offices filled with rows upon rows of desktop computers, blank screens staring back at him lifelessly. But no people.

Then he reached the far office, saw that a soft light left the door window, and heard the muffled, rapid tapping of keys from within. He rapped the window with his knuckles.

'Da?' came a shrill reply.

Lior opened the door. He stood in the entrance to the office looking down at a lithe man with dark rings beneath his eyes, hands resting on a computer keyboard. He looked Lior up and down, clocked the uniform and the ID.

'Chego tee khochesh?' *What do you want?*

'Are you the boss?' replied Lior.

'What does that matter?'

'My boss told me that I need to speak to the person in charge about temporarily shutting off power to this building. He said they should know about it.'

'That's ridiculous, we're working around the clock trying to salvage as much data as we can and you want to shut the damn power off. Perfect, absolutely perfect.'

The man pushed back from the desk and got to his feet. 'This better be the illustrious Boris forgetting to tell me something again and not your screw up otherwise you can forget it.'

He pushed past Lior and darted down another length of corridor, muttering to himself. Lior watched him disappear into another office and then he turned to look at the man's desk, at the screen, at the tables of data on the walls, anything to help him understand what information they were hoping to salvage.

'He must be in the control room.'

The man had reappeared from another office and looked up to see Lior eyeing his desk. 'That's classified information,' he said coldly. Lior half-heartedly withdrew his gaze from the office. 'You better come with me upstairs to get this straightened out.'

And so they took three flights of stairs at a gallop, the man pulling his body around each handrail with a yank, his feet striking the steps with surprising agility. At the top of the stairwell they pushed through swing doors into a control room. Steel shelving held lifeless computer servers, and cabinets against the painted breezeblock walls contained folders of ageing paper. At the far end, a late middle aged man sat beneath the only light in the large space, hunched over a printer spewing out a series of numbers and letters dispersed in a rhythmic pattern, up and down a continuous gridded roll of paper.

'Wait here,' the younger man said, and so Lior stood by the door, eyes playing over the tangle of wires, papers and posters of star systems covering the walls.

The skinny man mumbled to the other, who Lior presumed was Boris. After studying the room, Lior directed his full attention to trying to listen to the conversation between them. He heard, 'I'll just call security.'

Lior swept towards them, crossing the open plan control room, and almost clashed with Boris as he stood and turned. He was a hulk of a man in his lab coat, with great glassy eyes, spidery veins across his cheeks and thin reading glasses balanced on the crown of his head. He looked straight at Lior in intense bafflement, stepped back and said, 'I'm afraid I have no recollection of this at all, not at all. And it would be most inappropriate.'

The younger man had reached a telephone receiver and held it to his ear, a finger poised on the number pad.

Lior looked between them.

'Well, what have you got to say for yourself?' Boris suddenly demanded.

'I'm not here about the power. I'm here because … because I need to talk to you. Alone. Don't call security. I'm not here to harm anyone. I want to talk to you about your computers being hacked.'

'What could you possibly know about it? Who are you?' The younger man still hadn't replaced the telephone receiver. Boris joined him in watching Lior closely.

'I know about it because I did it.' He let the information sink in before he continued, 'But once in, all I did was check that I could open a file, that I had full admin rights. But the damage to your servers … to me. I didn't get something into your network, I let something out.'

They watched him with growing suspicion.

'And that something got into here.' His index finger ran

across his forehead, moving aside a tuft of hair, to his temple. He removed the cap over the wetchip port: a black hole encircled by a silver ring the width of his finger.

'This guy is nuts.'

'Do you have any other idea about how we managed to lose a decade of work, Mikel?' Boris responded.

Mikel was silent.

'I suggest —' he paused and looked at Lior, eyebrows raised.

'My name is Lior.'

'I suggest, Lior, that you continue.'

'This is a wetchip port —' Lior started.

'I have seen one before,' Boris said. 'A computer scientist in St Petersburg. Are they safe?'

'They're still in beta testing, but I'd used mine for months without a hitch. Now though …'

'What could have possibly come from this station,' Boris indicated to Lior's head, 'and into your wetware port?'

'You have to know,' Lior glared at Boris intensely. 'You did this to me. Why is this place here? What research do you do?'

'Isn't it obvious,' Mikel answered, 'this is a radar station covering the Arctic in case missiles start flying across the ice following your recent exploits —'

'That's enough,' said Boris.

'Oh come on. He killed Yegor and Vladimir, and destroyed everything we have worked on over the past ten years, half the world is looking for this man and you're humouring him, Boris. We need to call the guards and get him in front of the FSB, not this kangaroo court.'

'And they take him away and will, in turn, ask us what he did to cause all of this. So I ask again, Mikel,' Boris was seething now and purple in the face, 'do you have any idea what happened, or shall we use this opportunity to try to find out?'

Silence.

'Why don't you sit down, Lior,' Boris gestured behind him, the colour draining from his face. 'You look like you've been on quite a journey.'

He indicated to an old leather armchair beneath a giant map of the northern hemisphere's constellations. Above that, glass skylights framed a crystal clear night sky, sparkling with the faint glow of our galaxy behind a scattering of less distant stars. As they walked towards some low seating, Mikel stayed at the desk for a few moments. He put down the telephone receiver and tapped a few keys on the computer before coming over to join them, perching on the edge of a terminal on the other side of the room.

'I'm sorry about the two men, your colleagues,' Lior said. 'I didn't mean any of this. I'm here because I want to know what happened. Why do you have the quantum supercomputer?'

'I think a more pertinent question is, why on earth were you hacking into our network?'

Lior took a breath. 'It doesn't matter anymore … it was an idea, its time has passed. I wanted to use some of its memory and processing, but as I said, I didn't get that far.'

'That's the reason?' Mikel said. 'That's the reason they died?'

'Why should we trust you?' said Boris. 'How are we meant to know you're not here to sabotage the station even further? That you don't work for a foreign secret service. The radar is now back up and running on temporary systems so you've come to finish the job?'

'Look, to start with, I wouldn't be talking to you. If you feel that you can't tell me something then don't. But quantum supercomputers are all over the planet now. Were you creating some kind of artificial intelligence, is that it?'

Boris sat back and held up his hands.

'Just the two of us? Far from it. It's here for two reasons: it's cold and it's far from any major cities. It lies many storeys beneath the camp, and was maintained largely by an automated system. As well as Yegor and Vladimir of course, although they mostly worked on the pumps…'

He glanced over at Mikel, who folded his arms and stared at the floor.

'Anyway, we occasionally schedule the use of a tiny fraction of its processing power,' Boris continued. 'So it's networked to our servers here. But it's largely unused as far as we know. We're told that it's for contingency purposes. Unless our political masters were using it from Moscow before you severed the net link to the station. All files to do with the radio telescope were held on servers in the basement, or in the folders around you.'

He gestured with a sweeping arm at the steel shelving containing hundreds of paper files against the walls of the large room. Some of the paper pushing out from the edges of stuffed cardboard boxes had yellowed with the passing of the years.

'In fact, since the incident, we've had to go back to filling these folders with our records.'

'Records of what? You still use this old thing?' Lior pointed up, his elbow resting on his knee.

'Of course. It may be over eighty years old and built to track American satellites but it does the job. We scan for asteroids heading our way, study quasars, listen to HabStars, and the Kremlin pretty much leaves us alone. Well, they did.'

'Then the file I opened, it could have been from space, from a military satellite maybe?'

Boris paused, his eyes still on Lior's.

'Can you remember anything about the folders or drive the file was in? Any words or diagrams maybe.'

'I can recall strings of numbers and random letters like normal people can recall a name. The file was called 00-594-37-61V-140603- 20010305.'

Boris didn't move. It was if time had stopped, and if they listened carefully they might have heard snowflakes landing on the frozen ground outside. The darkness of the room closed in around the lamp arched over the workstation, swallowing them.

'Who are you really?' Boris said finally, breaking the silence.

'I am a nobody originally from Ukraine who has now marked himself out for certain capture and imprisonment at the very least. And permanent deformity.'

'Deformity?' Boris's eyes narrowed.

Lior hesitated, then pulled up his right sleeve, bearing the upper part of his arm where a deep cut had not completely healed. And there, a centimetre or two along from his elbow joint, he pushed apart scar tissue to reveal a silvery metallic cord where a white organic tendon should have been. But the ridge beneath the skin of the remainder of his arm matched up with it perfectly. Then Lior hissed and grit his teeth trying to close the cut as a dark fluid oozed from it like blood. He took a rag from his pocket, already blotted with what was either this dark liquid or oil, and wrapped it around the wound tightly, holding it up, his elbow perched on the back of his chair.

Mikel had watched all this with a mix of astonishment and horror. Boris, however, had just made contact with an intelligence beyond this world, and in his eyes, he now looked upon proof finally of the existence of a second genesis. He dared not breathe in case he should awaken from a dream.

CHAPTER TWENTY-ONE

'Mikel, find 61 Virginis,' Boris said, almost whispering. Mikel lingered on the spot then drew himself away to another workstation.

'It's a star isn't it?' Lior asked. 'Where the code's from. I've got something in my brain from another star system. And now it's infecting me, turning me into something else. Something not even human.'

Boris stared at Lior with the look of a man about to talk to a ghost. 'Do you feel different? Apart from your body. Different in your mind? Why are you here? Do you have a message for us?'

'Stop speaking to me like I'm something other than who I am. Everything I know, I've already told you.'

'Who are you?'

Mikel swung around to them from the computer terminal. 'Nothing currently out of the ordinary.'

'What was the date of the file?' Boris asked Lior. 'What were the last eight digits?'

'20010503.'

'So the signal was recorded on the third of May 2001.'

'Mikel, check the folders.'

'The folders go back to 2020. Everything before then has been archived. It'll take a few days to get hold of them.'

'But why wasn't it detected at the time?' asked Lior. 'Why has no one else picked it up? How could it have just sat on your servers? It must have been copied from one server to another since then and yet it hasn't escaped.'

Boris shrugged his broad shoulders and turned out his hands. 'Back at the turn of the century we just didn't have the computing power to look very deeply at the data for weak signals, or at a large class of signal types. That's why the SETI at home project started, using the net to take advantage of computers doing nothing all over the world. So it could have been overlooked. There's so much to go back over. We need to get the files. I don't know. I didn't get here until around 2015. In any case, it sat on a server until you opened it, uncompressing it probably.'

'Why would they send a signal of a code that corrupts every computer system it infects?' Lior said. 'No 'we come in peace', just the most devastating computer virus ever made.'

'Well, to send a question back will take around, what?' Boris looked at Mikel. 'Twenty-eight years so we might have to wait a while to find out.'

'Twenty-seven point nine,' Mikel said.

'Incredible that it arrived as it has,' Boris went on. 'Signals weaken over distance of course, but this must have been a focused, amplified transmission to allow for interstellar degradation. In any case, we must send something. I may not live to witness a reply, but you might.'

Boris leant back against a desk, his eyes still wide but now unfocused on the space in front of him – the palm of his hand over thick lips hanging open in wonder.

'Twenty-eight years', he repeated. 'Twenty-eight years …'

A warning siren rang out through the camp in a droning wail. Its eeriness was disquieting. Boris stood and walked to the window.

'That means the camp is being locked down,' he said,

looking out into the night. 'Guards are heading this way. Running.' Boris looked back at Mikel. 'Did you tell them he was here?'

'No, you saw me – I put the phone down before I touched a button.'

Boris stared at him. 'You sent them a message, didn't you?' Mikel didn't move. Then his lips pursed together.

Lior looked at him, then at Boris.

'Mikel,' Boris roared. 'You utter fool.' Mikel shrunk and stared at the floor.

Boris turned to Lior. 'I'm sorry. Let me help you. You can hide.'

Lior could see in his eyes the marvel of what stood before him. He could hear the honesty and truth of what he said. He longed to stay, to learn more. To heal. But this Mikel had robbed him of that. A panic rose through his legs and gripped his stomach.

They could hear the main doors to the building slam open below. Boris and Mikel eyed the door to the stairwell and then looked at Lior.

He watched them. Now there was nothing more he could take from them, nothing more could be done. He forced a strength into his body, to still it.

He said, 'No one on this planet can help me, and now no one else can be helped. Life as we know it might end, and the stars above will burn brightly.' He turned towards the door.

'No. Wait,' Boris burst away from the window and ran to grip Lior's shoulders. 'You can stay here, I won't tell anyone who you are. There must be a reason for this. There must be more we can learn from you.'

'Get off me,' Lior stepped away from him. 'I'll be in an interrogation room by morning. Then dissected. Then perhaps I'll wake up to a nuclear winter with everyone else.'

He moved away but this time Boris put his great arm around Lior to turn him from the door.

'No, you can't leave. The world must know of you. Maybe even see that there is no sense marching towards war if there is other life out there. You change everything.'

Lior could hear the stampede of boots on concrete stairs from beyond the door.

'I would have thought not knowing if there is any other life beyond this world makes it even more important that we avoid destroying what could be unique. But that hasn't helped us, has it?'

With a spin, Lior shoved Boris away.

'And I fear it is too late for people to stop the mobilisation of nuclear warheads because a man knows the name of a file and has synthetic fibres in his arm. Thank you for knowing where the code came from. I'm sorry it came to this.' And with that, he swept out of the room into the stairwell.

Looking over the rail he could see two soldiers turning up the final flight of stairs. They saw him and one shouted, 'Stand still.'

Lior ignored them. Instead, he looked back to Mikel standing in the middle of the radio telescope control room, and a dishevelled Boris joining him to watch aghast, then he turned and kicked open the steel window frame facing south, back to the main gate. The lock snapped beneath his heel. Lior leapt out into the night, his tattered black raincoat fluttering in the icy air behind him.

Lior dropped off the end of the entrance roof, down to the

car park. The Gazprom van was hidden from view beneath it. As he was reversing out, a soldier appeared at the main door to the building and roared, 'Stop or I fire.'

Lior shifted the transmission to drive, then hit the accelerator. The vehicle arced away from the building and he dropped sideways onto the grey fabric passenger seat and drove blind. The car windows exploded, sending shattered glass all over him, and deafening rounds ricocheted off the metal frame, pinging off in all directions. He bounced over what must have been a kerb and pushed himself back up to sitting. He could see the main gates two hundred metres or so in front of him, down the central road.

Then a round hit him in the back.

A shockwave punched through the flesh above his kidneys and thumped up against the inside of his ribcage. He made a guttural noise in agony, let his eyes roll back into his head as he arched away from the burning hole in the seat. Blood welled up into his mouth and nose before he coughed it out over hands still gripping the wheel. His legs had extended with the pain, forcing the accelerator into the floor.

His vision blurred so that the main gates sped towards him as if he were in a tunnel, streetlights streaking past, the wind roaring in his bloody ears. And now, as the gate guard knelt and took aim, deafening rounds screamed past him. He could do nothing to move his focus off the padlock on the barbed wire gates. Beyond, snowy trees were lit up in brilliant white from the perimeter floodlights, and he moved towards the light as if in a nightmare, accelerating uncontrollably.

In what could have been seconds or a lifetime, he had scattered the kneeling soldier and thundered into the centre of the steel bars. The padlocked chain snapped in a ferocious whip that clipped the side of his face and knocked him against the door. The door flung open as the vehicle skid horizontally down the icy road and Lior was thrown when the tyres hit the low embankment. Landing in a snowdrift helped numb the white pain coursing through his nerves. He could have blacked out momentarily, he wasn't sure. But his eyes opened and fixed themselves on the treeline and the darkness beyond the glowing canopy.

Then the floodlights turned off, plunging everything into darkness, and Lior knew that he had half a chance. Maybe not to live but to escape capture, so as not to spend his final hours or days being dissected and studied, but free, on his back in the cool powder looking up at the stars, at 61 Virginis, wondering whether the beings there had lives very different from those on Earth, or if they too suffered.

He lifted his head, and shuffled himself onto an elbow, then ignored the agony and inability to breathe and rolled onto all fours. He found himself staring down at the shadows of a bloody impression in the snow the shape of his head. He could see the greys and faint hue of rouge in greater detail than he thought possible. And lifting his head, the pitch-black field before him and the trees, illuminated only by starlight, lay bare their every indentation and tuft of grass in a clear silvery-blue.

A blizzard was coming down now. He rocked forwards and one foot found traction beneath him, then the other, and he stood, swaying slightly as his head drained of blood. Looking over his shoulder, over the wreckage of the van, he watched three guards canter out of the trembling gates still swinging on their hinges fifty metres away. Then he looked back at the trees and stepped towards them. Finding that he could walk, he tried to break into a run.

In the few inches of new snow across the wide but frozen

grassland, he found that if he watched for the tufts and snowdrifts he could move at a steady but fragmented jog. And so, drawing wheezing, bloody breath that burnt his lungs, and pushing through the piercing pain searing through his torso and fractured skull, he thrashed onwards away from the road.

He could hear shouting behind him, then, as he reached the trees almost drained of life, the bloodthirsty barking of protection dogs that evidently could smell his scent on the wind. He looked back to see terrifying silhouettes of Dobermans being let off their leashes in front of the van's headlamps. He saw the hunger with which they pelted the ground towards him.

Lior dug inside of himself, grunted and plunged through the surrounding foliage. In the forest it became more difficult to see, and he stumbled over tree roots until the ground dropped away beneath him. His vision died. His legs gave way. He tumbled onto his side and found himself sliding through low pine branches that tore at the remainder of his face. That discomfort turned to the definite sensation of teeth clamping around his right arm, and the wet smell of stale meat drifting into his nostrils. His last thought was of his mother, and he prayed for her.

Then he wasn't aware of anything at all.

CHAPTER TWENTY-TWO

Boris, sitting on a collapsible steel chair in a dark, cold and otherwise empty cell in the station guardroom, let his thoughts drift to the beginning of his time as a radio astronomer. To when he was still a young man, full of zeal and optimism for the future, for the investigation of the universe and certain discovery of other intelligent life within it. Years had passed. He had married then divorced. Lost his only son to a tumour.

All the while, he had listened, he was always listening. But wherever he was on that fateful day when contact was made, he was not in the radio telescope to hear it. No one was. A streak of electromagnetism, a band of light not visible to our eyes, had traversed a vast emptiness and found only computer storage. Now old and tired, tired of his lonely existence, tired of the world, he finally knew that life had started on another planet, and therefore finally he knew, not believed, but knew that the universe was teeming with it. Earth was not unique. It was not special. The grouping of molecules to form a cell, a single cell that gave rise to all life on this planet, our last universal common ancestor – a grandparent shared by every human, every orchid, every wild boar, every bacterium – was not a one-off event. And just as cells form our being, beings an interplay of ecosystems that are unsustainable alone.

But this wonder – our life, the life of the organism that is Earth – is nothing but a fraction of thousands upon thousands of other ecologies, perhaps millions upon millions. Lives lived out elsewhere, some sapient though perhaps oblivious, or perhaps well aware, of what Boris now knew. And so he waited, thinking so many thoughts he had waited his life to savour, as war beckoned, and an instrument of it touched down on the central square.

Rotor-blades whipped snowdrifts up into great billows of powder, which swept past the narrow, metre-length grate running along the top of his cell wall, a grate just wide enough to fill the dank space with a faint light so that Boris could see mould on the bricks around him and his breath condensing on the violently cold air. He looked up at the strip of metal. Through it, all he could see was brilliant white.

A deafening clang made him start. The door bolt retracting from the wall reverberating the two-inch steel momentarily before the door swung open, cracking against the brickwork. One of the guards stepped in and stood in the corner of the room, his rifle levelled at Boris. Behind him strode two severe men in black, full-length, woollen coats, black leather gloves, black polished shoes.

One had shaved his dark receding hair almost to the root, which, with sunken eyes and a damaged nose, gave him the look of a boxer. The other was older, greying and sporting a trimmed moustache beneath beady eyes which glared at Boris like a hawk eyeing prey. They both moved with frightening economy and purpose, squeaking shoes slapping the concrete floor and echoing around the room in a shrill and menacing cacophony of noise, that grew overwhelming with their approach.

Then it stopped. The larger man stood with his hands held at his side, behind the hawkish one who stood obliquely to Boris in the middle of the room, hands behind his back, looking up at the strip of sky. There was a sudden stillness, and silence, which felt crueller than the rapid movement and noise. After a few seconds of waiting for someone to say something, Boris stirred. He pushed back to sit upright, and the chair scraping over the floor pierced the quiet. But still, neither of the visitors moved.

Then the older man spoke without shifting his gaze from the grill or what lay beyond it. His voice was clipped, hard and without warmth.

'There are many things about the circumstances I have been told of, that I do not understand. I understand you have been harbouring a terrorist. The one responsible for the shutting down of this establishment, and the killing of many of your countrymen in Ukraine. Why would you, a government employee, do this I wonder? And why did he come here, all the way from the United Kingdom? But most of all, I wonder why I have been sent here, to this desolate place, to speak to you about it, to discern the truth of the matter. It is most strange. In any case, the first question concerns you, and as you are here, that is where we shall begin.'

He turned and stared into Boris.

'Why did you not alert the guards as soon as you realised he was here? And why did you act to protect him?'

'He is not a terrorist.' Boris met his gaze. 'He was a hacker, not wanting to destroy anything.'

'It is in your interest that you do not make me repeat my questions.'

Boris took a deep breath then let it exhale slowly, filling the space in front of him with its vapour. He waited until it had dispersed, before he began.

'It is going to be difficult for you to believe this, but he opened a file we had, a signal containing a code from another star system, a code that got into his head and which he now carries within his wetware or nervous system. He is the only evidence of extra-terrestrial life on Earth, and he is not dangerous. That is why I saved him.'

'Tried to save him, Dr Krakow; the dogs got him last night. The snow will have buried him now and, as I understand it, a search for the body has been unsuccessful. There are no heat signatures in the woods, no sign of him having left the tree line on satellite imagery.' He looked over his shoulder at the guard who nodded at this. 'The dogs stayed with him long enough to drench their gums and teeth in blood before even they could not stand the cold. Your evidence of extra-terrestrial life, as you call him, is no longer living.'

He let the words echo around them one at a time quite deliberately, and the bigger man smirked watching Boris register each one, face limp, eyes opaque and drained of strength.

The FSB officer went on. 'Which is unfortunate, as we could perhaps have used his obvious cyber-warfare skills in the coming days.'

'You people are sick warmongering imbeciles, without the faintest concept of your puny existence. There is such life here on Earth, and infinitely more beyond, and yet you merely wish to destroy it. How stupid, how ignorant and how small-minded of you.'

'I'm afraid that being so detached from life has left you with little understanding of the balance of power in this world that affords you the freedom and resources to look at the sky all night. A freedom that must be backed by the threat of force, or else someone will take it. It has always been like this, and likely always will. Most unfortunately. And so, Dr Krakow, this is why I have my associate with me. So that you will tell me everything you know of this 'hacker', sparing the little green men nonsense. Did he tell you who he was working for? Has he initiated any other attacks on us? And did he tell you anything that will help us defend ourselves against or attack the West?'

'I wouldn't tell you even if I knew the answer to any of those questions. But in themselves, they are insignificant by many orders of magnitude, and you are a fool.'

The associate moved across the room at a frightening speed and connected his leather bound knuckles with Boris's nose, exploding it while simultaneously throwing him backwards off his chair so that he landed flat on his back on the concrete floor. As he landed, steel toecaps started swinging into his ribs and continued to do so with sickening, unceasing brutality.

From the same window he had seen Lior leap through only hours before, Mikel now watched the helicopter take off from the square beside the guardroom. He studied the one cell window that he had seen shadows play over during the visit. Now there was no sign of movement.

After the sky was once again a washed-out stone colour and he couldn't tell whether the hum he could hear was the sound of rotor blades or the control room terminals behind him, he left the window, made his way down the stairs and shuffled through the snow towards the cells.

'Boris,' Mikel whispered, huddled against the bare brick wall beneath the horizontal slit of metal grate.

'Boris, are you there?'

Mikel looked around nervously, anticipating the sound of snow crunching beneath combat boots. He strained, listening for a reply.

'Boris … it's Mikel.' He looked up at the grill. Blew into his hands. He looked like death: white as a sheet with dark circles beneath his swollen eyes.

Then a croaking, weak voice found its way through the thin air, 'What do want?'

'Boris. Are you well? What did they do to you?'

'What do you care?'

'I didn't mean for any of this to happen. I'm sorry, Boris. I thought he was a spy, or special forces.'

Silence.

'He's dead, Mikel. They killed him.'

'He could have killed us.' Mikel was visibly upset now, his eyes glistening with the shame and the cold. 'How was I to know?'

There was silence.

Eventually, a sigh.

'You weren't, Mikel.' Silence again. Mikel looked up at the grill.

'But you can still find him. If you don't find him he'll be completely buried. Perhaps unrecoverable.'

Mikel's eyes gained resolution. He nodded to himself, and definition crept into his previously slack and gaunt face.

'I will. I will find him.'

'You must go, before they see you.'

'But are you going to be OK?'

'I'll live.' A wince of pain found Mikel's ears, making him grimace.

'Now go,' Boris commanded.

Mikel turned and scampered away from the wall and back

onto the road. He resumed a walking pace, but one that was rapid and determined, very different to his hobble there.

Retracing his steps towards the radio telescope, and his 4x4 truck beneath it, Mikel knew that soon the camp would be investigated again, or else there would be war, and so he had little time to lose before evidence of his civilisation, and potentially another, was confiscated or annihilated forever. If ever there was a moment to redeem himself, Mikel decided, this was it.

CHAPTER TWENTY-THREE

Four days later, in a draughty fifteenth-century Orthodox monastery, Mikel knelt in its cathedral, his hands clasped on the back of a wooden pew. The light from a hundred candles bathed him in a soft glow, surrounded by sharp shadows stretching upwards from chiselled stone columns to the cloisters several stories above. A stained glass depiction of Christ's resurrection towered over him, the colours iridescent.

Having prayed for the third morning in a row, Mikel had become accustomed to the soreness in his knees, the smell of musty oak and charred wicks, and flickering movements about him from darting candlelight. Now he could, for the first time in his life, lose himself in asking for penitence.

It was a transcendent feeling, a sensation of being lifted up from his crude and earthly self and embraced by light. He felt, if not free of responsibility, forever welcome to momentarily put it down, to lighten his load and rest for a while. This was perhaps the overriding value in accepting God's love: the comfort of knowing that one's life, whatever may pass, is in His hands; and then in death we too are lifted from the otherwise brutal unknown, or rather, unknowable.

Mikel had watched Boris kneeling close to where he was now, whilst he sat on a pew at the back of St Nicolas Cathedral. His car had broken down five or six years ago, and Boris had asked to stop for ten minutes on the way back from the station. Just to light a candle for his son, he had said.

Then he became lost in prayer.

Behind Mikel, down a long, dark hallway, the main door to the monastery opened and a hooded figure stepped inside. The door closed as gently and swiftly as it had opened, and the individual slipped silently into the shadows.

Delphi crept along stone corridors listening for the sound of footsteps following her. She had caught a glimpse of the lit pews and altar as she had entered and quickly hid from view to avoid being seen by early morning worshippers.

The monastery was largely open to visitors, with a small shop due to open in a few hours, a museum and gallery extending into one of the wings. The living quarters were on the other side of a large, paved courtyard, where a few lights were twinkling through slits of windows in the carved stone as monks began their morning routines. Towering over it all were the five-domed towers of the cathedral in vibrant blue and yellow.

In the wing furthest from the entrance lay what she was looking for: the infirmary. Peering around the corner of the corridor, she could see a monk sitting at an old wooden desk beside a glass-panelled door. He had speckled skin, illuminated by a hovering spherical glow lamp beneath which he was completing a paper report.

Delphi stepped backwards into a cove beside a supporting column, and with her hood pulled low over her eyes, waited in the darkness for the inevitable.

After what she estimated to be twenty minutes, she heard the scraping of chair legs against the stone floor, and then the soft padding of the monk's footsteps as he walked towards her. She sunk back into the wall and held her breath. The monk shuffled past her with his head lowered, scanning the floor, holding the glow lamp in his hands delicately like a flower.

He turned towards the third doorway on the right. It opened gently away from him and he stepped through onto the newly-tiled lavatory floor. When the temporary glow faded back to the darkness of the seemingly endless corridor Delphi concluded that the door had closed. She drew a sharp intake of breath and padded around the corner, past the desk and through the glass panelling.

She found herself amongst antique medicine cupboards and filing cabinets. The smell of cleaning products, pharmaceuticals and stale fluids pricked her sinuses. She walked carefully, dim lighting above a fire escape only just illuminating large items of furniture as fuzzy shapes in the murkiness of dawn. From the silence emerged a steady electronic beeping in the distance. And then, beyond a shelving unit which extended out perpendicular into the long room, pinpricks of red and green lights hovered in the gloom at the far end. White sheeting appeared to cover a body.

Delphi glanced behind her, but the desk and the monk were out of sight and nothing moved. Through the slits of windows the horizon was brightening slowly, but it was as good as night around the monastery.

She walked swiftly, a tension rising from her twisted-stomach, tightening her chest so that her breathing was swift. The hairs on her forearms stood on end. She had refused a call to leave Russia so that she could find Lior. She had risked everything. In front of her, a drip and wires from an electrocardiogram descended onto the bed. Stepping closer, she could see that the sheet was not covering the individual's head, but instead bandages were wrapped around the near side of the face and scalp.

Beside the bed, she leant over and looked down at the exposed half of the face, and with its high cheekbones, narrow nose and – even in unconsciousness – a certain dignity. Instantly she knew it was him.

The sound of ruffled fabric alerted her to the presence of someone approaching from the entrance to the room. She turned, expecting the on-duty monk to be ambling towards her with a panicked look and blasphemy on the tip of his tongue.

Instead, as fast as the wind, a steely figure caught her by her throat and ripped her across the room and into the far wall. The stone caught the back of her head with a crack, sending an excruciating pain through her skull and darkening her vision as consciousness ebbed.

The gloved hand at her neck tightened its grip so that she could not breathe, and agony spread from her head to her throat and then down into her lungs as they strained for oxygen. A frantic panic set upon her and she looked up into the expressionless eyes of a man just doing his job. His chestnut irises, vulnerable beneath a mousy fringe, helped turn fear into anger, and she stabbed clawed fingers towards them.

He caught her wrist then immediately pulled her head away from the wall before smashing it back against the stone with his forehead. She let out a groan this time, his grip releasing her throat to let her skull take the full force of the impact.

Her legs crumpled and she fell to one side. He knelt and slipped a wire noose over her head. She felt it slide down over her forehead and nose, but just as it tightened over her larynx, she drew a hand under it and clenched a fist. The operative gripped her temple with one hand and yanked the cord with the other.

In the darkness, she thrashed around and garbled, seemingly desperate for breath.

After half a minute or so she slowed her struggle, letting her body go limp. She dared not breathe, and drew in on herself, calming her heartbeat, slowing her metabolism.

A few seconds later the man released the cord, wrenching it from her head as he rose from his knees to standing. Delphi lay still in the darkness. She had to do something but fear kept her where she was without a plan. She was a few feet from Lior finally but unable to protect him. Eventually, she began to crawl away, slowly, silently. There must be a scalpel on a cabinet. A toolbox with a hammer or chisel in it. Anything.

The man moved further into the room, towards Lior.

Delphi had made it past three beds, back towards the entrance to the room, when her wrist caught the wheel of a trolley, dislodging it with a squeak on stone. The sudden rush of fabric from beside Lior's bed and sharp footsteps marching towards her, told her everything she needed to know.

She scrambled onto her knees and was clambering onto her feet when the lighting turned off in the corridor ahead of her and the ECG beeping went silent. It was pitch black suddenly, the night enclosing them. She hesitated for a moment, but then moved quickly to a large cabinet by memory and touch alone. She waited there, her back to it and to the room. She listened.

The footsteps had stopped.

Lior rose from his bed. He watched the stranger standing in the middle of the passageway. He could see him in a silvery-blue as clear as day. The man was looking directly towards him, in a slight crouch, his arms outstretched, head cocked slightly, as if listening. A pipe rattled faintly, spooking him and he whipped around towards the sound, one hand waving through the air anticipating contact. But none came.

Lior, with his bare feet and cotton gown, moved towards him without sound. Delphi's ultraviolet radiation formed her crouched outline at the end of the room. She was searching for something. She reached out and knocked an open cabinet door and it shook quietly, but in the pin-drop silence it sounded like thunder.

The man spun around and crept towards her. Reaching into his back pocket, he withdrew a blade – making a mess now was evidently not a concern.

Without warning, Delphi scrambled out from the cabinet and he rushed towards her. He was three meters away, the knife up and ready.

Lior's eyes widened and a sudden dread yanked at his heart. Then came rage and his eyes narrowed and his nostrils flared.

How dare you, he thought, and he shot down the corridor as quickly as a shadow. Like a bullet he tore into the assailant, who turning too slowly, only helped to expose his fleshy throat. The metallic ring finger on Lior's right-hand sliced through larynx as if it were cutting through a plume of smoke.

The man crumpled and spun onto his front with a thud against the unforgiving stone.

Delphi stopped and turned back. The lights in the corridor outside the infirmary came on again, bathing them in a cold light. She looked at Lior, eyes still wide in fear, and then at the man lying motionless on the floor beside him.

163

Then back at Lior.

An uncertainty, a bewilderment, crept into her face. She shook her head, her bottom lip beginning to quiver. They met each other, and embraced slowly, tenderly. She explored his face and an artificially rebuilt forearm, cool fingers playing over metallic tendons and plates. Lior felt that his right ear was missing, replaced by a conical indentation of metallic mesh.

She nestled her forehead against his, and then against the crook of his neck. He held her to him.

Standing there in the moments that followed, Lior wished that time would stop. Or that he could preserve perfectly each sensation, each feeling and impulse that coursed through him.

And then, as the intensity began to dissipate, and he found perfection slipping through his grasp the tighter he tried to hold onto it, he found that with the slightest intent he could, in his memory, bring back everything just as it was. Not just the passing moments but also everything he had ever experienced. And deep down, in his subconscious, began the stirrings of something more. Something that transcended his life, something that predated it. Something at once innately him, but also undeniably alien.

It was the unquestionable sensation of no longer being separate from the rest of the universe beyond his skin, but instead, inexorably a transient emergent system of the universe itself. Information. A pattern. That is all he was. All everything is. His mind was opening, uncompressing. Unravelling like packaged code.

Mikel heard a commotion and ventured down the central passageway to find the monk who had been keeping vigil of the infirmary standing motionless in the doorway, shaken and disturbed. They both stared in disbelief at Lior.

He stood with Delphi, dressed in a white nightgown, bandages lying in heaps at his feet. He had grown in stature, his frame filled out with synthetically enhanced tissue, which gave definition to his form. Most obviously his right forearm was predominantly a sleek, matt-grey collection of levers replacing bones, and cables and cylindrical motors replacing tendons and muscle fibres, all wrapped beneath metallic mesh. Only the underside of that arm, the edge of his hand and his index and forefinger remained flesh.

Lior, seeing them staring, flexed each of its digits and raised his arm in synchrony with his other so that they came to rest open in front of him. He came in peace.

He turned towards the monk, revealing the metallic mesh where a hole in the side of his head had been, and before that, his ear.

'Do not be afraid,' Lior began, his voice calm. 'This man,' he gestured towards the corpse on the floor, 'tried to take our lives and has paid with his own.'

The monk looked to the body and then back at Lior. He couldn't form a sentence.

Lior turned to Mikel.

'Please take us away from here.'

'My car is … parked outside,' Mikel said, stunned by what stood in front of him.

Lior collected his clothes from a cupboard beside the bed. Then, as they walked out of the room into the corridor, he laid a hand on the monk's shoulder.

'Thank you for your care. I have nothing with which to repay you other than my gratitude. And I am sorry about the body, but we must be on our way.'

165

The monk studied Lior's face, a hand over thin lips in thought.

'The Lord repays my devotion to him each second of every day. I require nothing more,' he said. 'As for this man, we will bury his flesh and let our Father judge his soul. As he will yours.'

CHAPTER TWENTY-FOUR

Mikel drove them straight to an airfield that Delphi had scoped out the day before, toeing the accelerator whilst glancing nervously in the rear-view mirror at Lior. On the way, Lior told Delphi about speaking to Boris and the star system. This news appeared to leave her dazed and afterwards he turned to watch the icy world go past the window in a new light. A pure, unbroken kind that seemed to be a fraction brighter and more saturated than the light in the world he had known before.

After a few minutes of silence, Delphi asked Mikel about how he had found Lior, and Mikel said that he had taken him for dead when he came across a foot sticking out of a thawing snowdrift after hours of searching by the barracks at dawn, before the guards did a daily sweep of the woods. Once he had uncovered the body, and was not able to hear breathing, he was about to leave and fetch a Skidoo to drag what he thought was a corpse to the road. But then, as he lay close to Lior's mouth, listening, he noticed the slightest amount of condensation on his glasses.

Sure enough, Lior was breathing faintly and his pupils reacted to the light when his eyelids were opened. Mikel heaved him over his shoulders and slowly carried him through the forest, resting regularly. At the forest track where he had left his car, he had slumped Lior onto the backseats and then driven to the monastery, where no one would think to find him.

'The snow concealed you,' said Delphi quietly, watching distant woodland. She looked at Lior and smiled. 'Even Earth is trying to protect you.'

They arrived at the airfield.

'I'm sorry,' Mikel said, looking up at the reflection of Lior in his rear-view mirror. 'I should have listened to what you had to say.'

Lior stepped out of the car, turned and held Mikel's arms, fixing him to the spot. He had attended silently to Mikel's recount of how he'd taken him to a place of sanctuary. He felt at peace. Pure. The debt had been paid. Mikel stared at him.

'Thank you for coming to my aid,' Lior said. 'Please now see that Boris is freed. I may need his help.'

Mikel nodded.

'The guardroom only had authority to keep him locked up for five days – he should be let out tonight. Although the FSB might return to continue the investigation.'

'Please see that he rests as I have,' Lior said, holding his gaze.

'He won't rest now. He has waited his whole life for this. For you. He'll likely be reporting the signal to SETI's Post-Detection Group and then working with other observatories to study the star system. But don't worry, we won't mention you.'

Mikel grinned, seemingly relaxed for the first time in Lior's presence.

'I only hope we have the time to listen and learn more,' Lior said, then he released his hold of Mikel, smiled, and walked towards the runway extending out to the horizon, open to the expansive sky.

Delphi found a local pilot she had met on her first visit to the airfield in the hanger completing post-flight checks of his aircraft. She paid him double his normal rate so that they could fly immediately and so that no questions were asked of Lior. She also bartered for one of the pilot's coats, a big cold-weather waterproof with a faux fur-lined collar. For three thousand rubles Lior could at least cover his arm and most of the side of his head beneath the hood.

'He'll be ready to fly in a few minutes,' Delphi said, after she had returned from the hanger to find Lior studying the cobalt coloured mountains on the horizon.

'Where are we going?' said Lior, inserting his synthetic arm into the sleeve of the coat.

'Copenhagen is the furthest the plane can go. I was hoping that after finding out about what happened at Vosinsk you would have an idea of what to do from there. All I had planned was to find you. To find out what had caused all of this.'

'And you did. I should never have left you.' He took her arms. 'I just didn't want to put you in any more danger.'

'I know. It's done. But what do we do now?'

'I have to show the UK what I have become. The Russians didn't do any of this. But let's avoid airport security. If we get a boat from Denmark there's less chance we'll be stopped.'

Delphi took hold of the coat's lapels and drew them together against the cold.

'Lior, the world is on the brink of war. We could go anywhere, hide anywhere. The farm we stopped at even, if they'll have us. Anywhere away from a city. Some life will survive – we'll rebuild.'

'What if humanity doesn't? We need to tell the planet that

the virus that triggered all of this wasn't an act of war.'

'You'll be taken into a laboratory and studied to within an inch of your life. They'll connect something to your wetware port, releasing the code and corrupting your nervous system in the process. Do you want that, Lior, after all you've been through, after all I've done for you, to just give up?'

'It's a risk I've got to take.'

'But you didn't start all of this, no one did. It's not your problem to solve anymore.'

Spotting the pilot emerge from the hanger, Lior looked away from Delphi, towards him, assessing, assimilating. But she continued. 'And if you want to keep running then go. I can fend for myself. But I don't want to. I don't want to be alone.'

Lior looked at her intently. In a world of uncertainty and an unfathomable number of eventualities, he knew deep within his gut that she was right. There was no reason to it. We act on our emotions, emotions evolved to deal with an unlit savannah, often with little relevance to the modern world. But they are all we have, and for the first time, Lior acknowledged that he wouldn't have it any other way. The pilot approached, but Lior's eyes stayed fixed on Delphi's.

'Neither do I,' he said eventually. 'You'll have to make sure they don't connect me.'

'Then you'd better stick with me from now on. We can go to a safe house in London. I've got a contact or two who can arrange a press conference. But let's fly from Copenhagen; there isn't much time, and I'll make sure there's a security clearance on your passport so we can slip straight through, trust me.'

He paused, then smiled. 'OK, I trust you.'

CHAPTER TWENTY-FIVE

In Copenhagen, Delphi booked a hotel so they could clean themselves up, replace their clothes and get some sleep before the next flight to London in six hours' time. Lior followed her from the street into a waiting lift, hands stuffed into pockets, hood pulled low over his face. They had a room on the seventh floor with windows that stretched from floor to ceiling and wall to wall, overlooking the lights of the city. Delphi pulled the curtains closed and turned back to Lior.

He stood in the middle of the room, arms now hanging by his sides, head crooked, eyes glazed over, fixed on a point on the floor, motionless. The metallic glint of the left side of his face drew her attention to where metal met his skin and how it was more of a lattice bond than a clean joint. The organic and synthetic meshed together.

His coat was stained with engine oil. His hair a tousled mess now with a higher hairline on the left side of his face. His right hand a slightly jagged but aesthetically humanoid replica, with spikes instead of his ring and little finger. He looked so alone and distant standing in the middle of a vast hotel suite, low table lamps creating pools of light around him in an otherwise dimmed and subdued room.

It exuded style with its teak floorboards, marble coffee tables, ebony chests and leather armchairs. In the centre of it all, Lior was all at once a libertarian rebel and a tall, mysterious traveller from a distant land.

171

'Can you get the … metal parts of you wet?' she asked him softly.

He looked up at her without any indication of being somewhere else entirely up until that moment.

'I was entombed in snow that thawed as Mikel found me, so it seems as though I am still waterproof, if that's what you mean? But I've started to regrow skin over the synthetic areas now like we said – I have … direct access to any system in my body.'

Delphi looked him up and down, astonished still at what he had become whilst cocooned beneath the snow. But she kept the tone light, playful.

'Good, because you need to have a shower. In fact, we both need to have a shower.'

Lior stood beneath the torrent of warm water and found it odd that his organic skin was so grateful for it. There was no easy explanation as to why, it was something he previously had not given much thought to, nor defined any further. Something that had little necessity or reason – it simply felt deeply gratifying. But now, as he turned his attention and awareness to it, he explored the rippling consequences of homoeostasis being achieved in a number of interwoven processes.

His muscles relaxed, his skin received soothing touch and his flesh warmed. Sensory nerves fired electricity up from the shell of his being into his brainstem and endorphins flooded his limbic system. He synthesised the functional protein units of β-endorphin molecules and released them in waves.

Delphi's soft eyes emerged from behind the door at the other end of the bathroom. He stopped and covered himself

172

with a hand whilst she continued walking towards him. She met his eyes at first, and then let her gaze play over his metallic arm and the tendons in his neck, which seemed to Lior to spread up into his head like the sepal of a flower. She stepped to his side, where his lower ribs and side of his abdominals had been supplemented by synthetic skeleton, tendon and muscle. Lior had concluded that the dogs must have been ravenous despite the cold.

Water ran in rivulets and continued down to the shower floor, hitting the stone with a steady patter. She at first touched his artificial hand, and gently took it to her face. His metallic fingers played over her cheek and danced across her lips. Then she ran her hands over his torso, exploring every indent and channel in the taut, metallic mesh.

He let her explore his body, fascinated by her interest, grateful for her acceptance of what to others might seem grotesque. As she caressed him, he studied the alien amendments to his body again and also found them beautiful. Then she took a loofah from his hand and washed his back, his arms, his chest.

She joined him in the shower and afterwards they made love on the white cotton bed. In the bedroom Delphi had not drawn the curtains closed over the city but instead let the sea of lights scatter around them. When she was not looking into his eyes, Lior could see she let her gaze rest on the reflections of their undulating and united bodies in the vast windows, studded with glints and superimpositions. Later she told him that she felt as though she had finally found someone who could make her feel complete. And as she had long suspected, it was not someone she could have found on Earth.

CHAPTER TWENTY-SIX

Later, whilst Delphi slept, Lior sat down in the lounge with a vodka and switched on an English language news channel on the wall display. He had missed days of events – at a time like this, it felt like a decade's worth. A studio presenter was reading an autocue about emergency meetings in response to the cutting off of diplomatic ties between NATO, Russia and its ally, China, as well as the chemical strike on India. India had not yet retaliated and was being placated by the US and other key allies.

Suspicions were that one jet of many, scrambled by Pakistan as a show of force against an Indian exercise taking place close to the border, had gone rogue, somehow becoming armed with chemical warheads in a pre-planned attempt by ISI officers to start a conflict with India. But then the presenter held a finger to her earpiece for a few seconds. She looked across the studio in astonishment in what seemed like an attempt to obtain some form of confirmation. She turned to the autocue once again and said gravely:

'We have just received some breaking news. In a conference which took place a few minutes ago, the Russian President has said that the entire Middle Eastern region less Israel … will be declared a war zone, with open hostilities beginning against any members of NATO armed forces left within the region at twelve hundred hours Meridian Time on the seventeenth of January. The President said that the ultimatum … and the potential for a limited war against US, UK and French forces if it is not met, is in direct response to the three countries' continued support of rebel groups within the region acting against Russian allies, and recent state-sponsored terrorism against Russian sovereign territory and its nationals, which it says is indicative of one hundred years of NATO expansion and aggression.'

Cue shots of the Kremlin, the White House, the Élysée Palace and 10 Downing Street. Reporters had already begun rushing to the locations ready for follow-up responses from the Presidents and Prime Minister. Whilst they waited, recent Russian footage of troop movements to its borders and the testing of missiles was replayed and the newsreader promised to update viewers with more information as soon as they obtained it.

Lior stood and took Delphi's phone out onto the balcony, where his conversation would be muffled by the glass doors and traffic below. He keyed in the Russian dialling code and then the number that had been taped onto the old-fashioned telephone on a workstation in the radio telescope at Vosinsk. Staring out towards the city hall, he let the connection ring, and ring, and ring …

Finally, someone picked up the phone. The voice was weak and rasping.

'Da?'

'Boris, it's me, Lior.'

'Lior.' His voice rose in intensity, then spluttered before continuing. 'Where are you?'

'It doesn't matter. Mikel said that you were beaten and interrogated. How bad are you? And why are you at the telescope at a time like this?'

'I'll live long enough to die of radiation sickness at least.

175

And they won't let me off camp so what else have I to do other than look at the heavens and pray?'

'So this is how it ends?' Lior responded. 'We discover that we are not alone in the universe and then we destroy ourselves. This is the answer to the Fermi paradox and there is nothing we can do.'

'I don't know. I think God always has a plan. There must be something to be done, otherwise how could 61V send us a code to stop it happening to us? It must be a pocket of civilisation that made it beyond this point, and is trying to help others. You have been sent here to save us.'

'But then why send only one?'

'Maybe it's unthinkable for a civilisation to have such primitive computing and yet create and use the bomb. Total war drove us to it before our time. Who knows? Perhaps they did send other signals.'

'It could just be an automatic message. The outer planets of 61V aren't inhabited, there's just a probe there, repeating signals to any system that gives off an unusual double-peak gamma signature. There could be millions of them spread throughout the galaxy, endlessly repeating a message from a civilisation destroyed millennia ago, perhaps by itself – it could be a last noble act of a people before they were extinguished … But then couldn't Earth just recover from the code anyway? There will still be pockets of computers not connected to the net. Not many, but enough for people to rebuild. Then it would start all over again.'

'Perhaps we are close enough now that we will learn,' Boris responded. 'Or perhaps the people of 61V are on their way here, following their signal, in order to show us the path to life beyond the filter.'

'There is another possibility,' Lior said after a while. 'They

176

could well be on their way here, yes – they could have been travelling for the last half-century. And what might they expect to find?'

Boris didn't speak. Lior answered for him: 'A defenceless world.'

'I … I cannot believe that.'

'We can only wait and see.' Lior looked up at the sky and found himself now able to observe a few stars twinkling softly in the otherwise cloudy sky. He thought of how far away those stars were and discovered that, for the first time in his life, he could imagine what it would be like to travel such a distance. Outside of the atmosphere – beyond this world – one would be surrounded by stars in all directions. No up, no down. Just emptiness and stars. He was lost for a few moments in rapture.

'Boris, I need you to help me,' he said eventually. 'I want to send a transmission to 61 Virginis, maybe tonight.'

Boris coughed, and winced at the pain of it.

'I'm not going anywhere.'

'Set up a continuous transmission from your workstation when I hang up, and I also need you to track a comms satellite in range of London.'

'What is this, an SOS for humanity?'

'I'll call in to see you soon, Boris. Thank you … for everything.'

Lior ended the conversation and looked out into the night, up at clouds lit by sallow light-pollution. An index finger encircled the circumference of his wetware port.

After many minutes, he decided to check through news reports on Delphi's phone to see if there had been further developments. There was nothing more than joint commitments to oppose any 'Russian aggression, or that of its allies'. Emergency meetings were underway with further announcements due later that night.

Then a piece on the BBC caught his eye, which linked to a page on previous brushes with World War III, a topic spreading like an epidemic across the net. It started with a picture of Tsar Bomba, the largest nuclear bomb ever detonated at about one thousand, five hundred times the combined energy of the bombs dropped on Hiroshima and Nagasaki. Lior drank in the scenarios within a second.

On the ninth of November 1979, computers at the North American Aerospace Defence headquarters indicated that a Soviet missile attack was underway, prompting US nuclear bomber crews to board their planes for take-off. But after a few minutes when satellite data failed to confirm any incoming missiles, US leaders decided against retaliation. It was discovered later that an operator had mistakenly inserted a tape containing a training scenario into an operational NORAD computer, imitating a full-scale attack.

Almost four years later, on the twenty-sixth of September 1983, a Soviet early-warning satellite indicated five US nuclear missile launches. An officer on duty had a matter of minutes to react, but deemed the readings a false alarm, concluding that more missiles would have been launched in the instance of a real attack. Later investigations revealed that, this time, satellites were to blame, mistaking sunlight reflecting off the tops of clouds for missile launches.

Many years later, on the twenty-fifth of January 1995, President Boris Yeltsin was awoken following a radar warning and subsequently activated a device to authorise nuclear launches. Again, a lack of satellite data avoided war.

And they went on. The number of circumstances in which total nuclear war on Earth was potentially moments away lent the possibility an ineffable eeriness given what would entail. It was absurd, surreal. Too difficult to imagine without elements of farce. And yet. And yet, in each case, someone had said no. Even with only minutes to spare, at first one lone individual, then perhaps others, steered all of humanity, and potentially all existing intelligent life, away from annihilation.

There had been, and would remain, hope.

When Lior finally lay beside Delphi, she rolled over and held him. She was asleep again within moments. Lior, on the other hand, lay motionless, staring out through the floor-to-ceiling windows.

Half an hour could have passed before he whispered to her, 'I don't want to die. I don't even want to live forever. I just want to be with you. I just want to run away and live a normal life, a good life. I want that more than I ever thought I'd want anything at all. More than I'd ever thought it possible to want something. I want you. Forever. Until the sun turns black.'

The flight from Copenhagen to London City Airport was battered by the storm which had been circling around Northern Europe for the last few weeks. Lior's appetite was not suppressed, despite Delphi having to clutch her armrest during one sudden plunge due to turbulence, and he ate his entire in-flight meal along with most of Delphi's.

His body had been sapped by aesthetic skin and tissue regrowth, so that he looked – apart from his grey irises – undeniably human. The synthetic parts of his body had set off the scanners at the airport, but Lior explained that he had had a number of operations and plates inserted following a car crash years earlier, before auto-drive cars had become widespread. Delphi's ID and the security clearance on Lior's Lithuanian passport had also helped reduce questions.

Through much of the flight Delphi was silent, and Lior thought about the life they might lead together if they had met earlier, or if they ran away together now and war was averted, or even if they survived a war, and lived to see what sort of world would rise from the nuclear winter. Would they be able to make a life together in somewhere like West Africa? Where temperatures might plummet, but be sufficient to sustain them living off the land, burning the great jungles.

But what a journey that would be, alongside so many others. Then there was the farmhouse in Russia, over two hundred miles from Moscow. If they travelled there Lior would be able to take his mother from the clinic en route. But what if she and Delphi succumbed to cancer or radiation sickness and he did not? How could he live with himself alone, knowing that he might have tried to avert war?

Soaring in across London, having left the storm over the sea, and whilst Delphi rested her eyes, Lior found that he could not answer that question, which puzzled him. He would rise above a broken people. They would be as if at the dawn of civilisation and he, more advanced than they could have envisaged even before the war, would be invulnerable, perhaps immortal. A thought he had barely dared himself to consider.

CHAPTER TWENTY-SEVEN

After being arrested and incarcerated in a room deep below the Thames, Lior now knew his journey from London to Russia and back had done more than just change his body and enhance his nervous system. It had made him question everything he thought mattered. Despite this, when Lior's interrogator pulled out a pistol and pointed it at his head he was drawn back into a normal perception of time. Evidently, self-preservation was still an instinct he had not lost.

Four other guards burst into the room and, as he turned to meet them, the muzzle of a handgun hit his temple. All he could see around him were the limbs of armed personnel in body armour, helmets and chest rigs.

He turned to escape but large hands grabbed and yanked the bolt between his wrists upwards. Another pair of hands and significant grunts were needed to pull his legs out from under him. His ankles were bolted again and he was hoisted up into the air. He thrashed around, arching his back and kicking his legs. But there were too many of them, and within a second he had been dumped onto a metal gurney. Straps whipped across his body and were fastened tight into his skin. Hands held him firm against the wipe-clean plastic. He was immobile, gagged, blindfolded, and fitted with a soundproof headset in seconds, and utterly at their mercy. He had never felt so terrified in all his life.

Now more than ever he had lost all control. But he

resisted the urge to scream with rage, and instead turned in on himself. Hopeless now, he decided to conserve his energy. And if this was the end, then at least he could spend his final few moments lost in the memories of the few times he had felt at peace. In his mother's arms as a child, or sprawled beside her on a grass verge beside a river. Laying in Delphi's embrace.

After what felt like five minutes, after he had been wheeled through corridors and entered and exited an elevator, they eventually arrived in a large room. Through fuzzy echolocation he knew there were perhaps five individuals in it, a series of waist-height tables surrounded by hard surfaces, and a door three tables from where he came to rest.

Bolts were loosened around him and he was slid, still strapped down, into a tube which was undoubtedly a multi-imaging scanner: Lior's eyes could pick out sheets of X-rays skimming up and down his body in blinding flashes of piercing white, and then magnetic fields arcing around him.

He was taken out of the tube and carried to a table. Bolts were drilled in around him. When the last one had been spun into place he felt his clothing being cut away from his body. After a few seconds, he was completely nude.

He felt like livestock: a piece of meat ready for butchering. In the dark he could have been in the children's home at dawn, beneath a blanket in his narrow room listening to the sound of piglets screaming before slaughter, their cries travelling on the still morning air from an abattoir across the river, silencing birdsong.

Like the specimen he was, Lior accepted the sudden probing of his skin. What he presumed were heart-rate monitors were attached to his chest and he felt a sharp object explore his metallic hand. Then devices were stuck equidistantly over his physique, and gloved hands prodded where synthetic alloys had repaired damaged regions. He could feel them, but the prodding was not painful. He felt a small electrical charge from one instrument and amplified it.

Bang.

The instrument sparked and blew apart in a flash of light and twisted, scorched metal, causing whoever was holding it to swear and drop it clinking to the floor.

The blindfold was removed and bright lights were flashed into his pupils by a female figure in white overalls. Unable to turn his head, Lior could only make out that he was in some kind of laboratory or surgery. The walls were tiled white, high-powered strip lighting illuminating everything in garish light. Metallic tools and instruments were lined up on a table beside him. Monitors and computer terminals on manoeuvrable stands were linked to the electrodes covering his skin.

The woman who had shone a torch into his eyes had walked over to join three other individuals in white overalls clustered around the screens, whilst one of them nursed a burnt hand beneath a running tap. He could see a multitude of images of his body – CTs, MRIs, ECGs, Ultrasounds – fused together in a three-dimensional model. As he had sensed, a network of wires appeared to have spread throughout his central nervous system, and already there were glimpses of it along motor nerves. The medical staff conferred, and then one with greying hair but an unnaturally blemish-free face left the room. Lior's eyes followed a junior member of the team as he glanced over to an adjacent wall. A large one-way mirror stretched along most of its length.

After a few minutes, the senior doctor returned to the room and spoke to the waiting group. Then they turned and looked at Lior. The greying man walked between them, padding slowly over to Lior with a dispassionate, featureless expression.

In his hand was a cable. One end was inserted into a tablet, the other ended in a wetware connection.

The doctor placed the palm of his hand on Lior's forehead. His dry skin was cold but surprisingly smooth. He stared down at Lior with cautious, penetrating eyes. Lior was wide-eyed with terror. For the first time since having the gag inserted into his mouth, he bellowed in outrage. He tried to wrench his head from the vice it was fastened in, but he could move only millimetres. The doctor watched him struggle indifferently, then seeing Lior's helpless vulnerability, his caution gave way to conviction. He dabbed a moist cotton bud on Lior's temple where an annular disc could just be made out beneath the skin. The area went numb. Then he raised the connector level and aligned it with the wetware port.

With another hand, he raised a scalpel.

But at that moment a high-pitched, screeching alarm rang throughout the lab and every corridor around them. Simultaneously, the lights went off before emergency lighting flickered into life above doorways, throwing cold blue onto polished medical equipment. After a second in which everyone remained motionless, icy water shot out of ceiling sprinklers, throwing the individuals about Lior into panic. He smiled in mirth and he relished the cleansing waters falling upon every inch of his exposed, tingling skin.

The doctor above him had pulled the wetware transmitter up beneath an arm to keep it dry, and he looked around in desperation. But there was no quick solution to all the electrical equipment being drenched. Nothing to reverse the testing being put back hours, if not days. So finally he hurried towards the exit, after the others seeking warmth and shelter from the torrent. He was the last one out and left the door ajar.

After a few seconds of falling water illuminated electric blue, Lior sent out electromagnetic fields from his hands. On the steel instrument trolley at his feet, a small rod, perhaps used to hold open wounds, rattled on the surface. Lior magnetised his right hand and the metallic rod slid across the table into his fingers. He quickly fed it through the strap over his wrist and then yanked it upwards so that it levered into the surface. The strap snapped. Lior had started to undo the strap over his other wrist when a silhouetted, hooded figure occupied the doorway. It paused there fleetingly then swept along the wall towards Lior, staying low just beneath the height of the tables, and came to his side. Water patted on the leather jacket and hood.

'Just sit tight,' said the figure, the voice muffled by the thundering rain. Hands were already undoing straps over his legs. 'I'll tell you when they're undone, then roll off the table this way and follow me, staying low.'

Lior had immediately identified Delphi's voice. It was as cool and impatient as ever. She pulled out his gag.

'What do you want?' he said.

'If only we knew,' she replied. Then the head-clamp disengaged.

'Let's go.'

She dashed across to the wall. Lior rolled off the table and moved to a cupboard where he took a lab coat and put it on. Then he followed her out of the room.

CHAPTER TWENTY-EIGHT

Lior and Delphi had passed through two doorways on their way to the central lift and stairwell when the sprinklers stopped. The main lights were still off, however, and the alarm was still deafening. They moved with a few individuals who were fleeing to the depths of the building, in the confusion paying no heed to a man wearing only a lab coat running amongst them.

Lior studied them carefully. As he overtook a man dressed in a suit he crashed into him, sending them both skidding through an open office doorway. Lior stood quickly and rose over the clean-shaven civil servant trying to push himself to his feet. Lior kicked him back to the floor. His silvery eyes shone in the darkness, and he snarled, 'Take off your shirt, trousers and shoes and get out.'

Delphi appeared in the doorway and the man hesitated. So Lior let his metallic, spiked transfiguration of a hand drag over the surface of a glass meeting table and stepped towards him. The glass screeched like fingernails on a chalkboard, leaving a jagged score in its surface and the skin on the end of Lior's finger split open. 'Don't test me.'

After the man had scurried away and Lior had changed into his shirt, trousers and black brogues, they left the room and made their way down the now empty corridors.

They were through the final security door when Jared stepped out from an office behind them. His pistol was clenched in a hand that swung loosely by his side, a suppressor screwed onto the muzzle. The alarm still shrieked.

Lior and Delphi were about to turn at a bend in the corridor. Jared watched them, his eyes scrunched together in a fury, sneering in disgust. He shook his head slowly, unbelieving. Lior took Delphi's hand as they neared the corner. Jared scowled, raised the pistol, took aim and squeezed the trigger.

Lior hit the floor hard. Delphi stopped and looked around as Jared strode towards them. She was in shock – her breath caught in her throat. A hook punch to her jaw sent her spinning into the wall, then crumpling to her knees. Jared paced over to her and hit her again. He started shaking her in a grief-stricken fury.

'How could you try to leave here with him, to be out in the open? Why would you decide that? What's wrong with you?' One hand held her throat whilst he slapped her around the head with his other. Smack.

'What is wrong with you?'

Smack. Lior's flying heel caught Jared in the side of his head and they went toppling through the open security doorway. The bullet had hit a synthetic plate that swept around Lior's ribs beneath his right arm, leaving only a flesh wound. Lior landed in a crouch in the middle of the corridor and stood slowly. Before him, further down the passageway, Jared was against the concrete wall, elbows keeping him from collapsing against it. He twisted his head as if trying to steady his vision. Then he looked up at Lior. He pushed off the wall and strode into the middle of the corridor, opposite him. They faced each other.

Lior's heart thumped in his chest, his palms sweating. Here he faced a man who had knocked him about like a puppet, a trained killer, an animal, who was now practically equal to him in size and weight. This was his chance to prove himself, as he had thought he might against the wolf. But instead, his insides had gone cold. The hair left on his skin stood on end, his limbs tingling with adrenaline. This was it: him or me.

Delphi had pushed herself onto her hands and knees, and now looked at them with a bloody eye and lips. Jared's pistol lay beside her. Then the internal computer system announced, 'Security lock-down in progress,' and Lior glanced around as a transparent and bulletproof security door slid into place across the width of the corridor, cutting them off from her. She was conscious, that was the main thing. She'd be OK.

He turned back to Jared, to the power-seeking individual in front of him. What he couldn't take with the threat of force he would take with violence itself. But at a cost. For in defending the realm, whatever realm that may be, we must on occasion take up arms, though never seek to increase our dominion. To do so merely increases the threat, and what a threat Lior had become.

'Why?' Lior said, his voice thundering over the alarm. 'You shot my father. You shot me. Why? What good has your gun achieved?'

Jared tightened his fists and looked Lior up and down.

'I should have killed you in Berlin, before we got to Gabriel, before Russia. Before war. Think on that.' He stepped forwards.

Lior steadied himself and raised a hand. 'Don't come any

closer. We can both walk away from this.'

'Who knows how else you might screw up Earth,' Jared said, stepping towards him, raising his clenched hands to his chest, tucking his chin down, hunching his shoulders, 'if I don't put an end to you now.'

He sprang forwards, wrapping his hand around Lior's wrist, exposing his flanks, and swept his free arm towards open ribs. Lior made to deflect the movement, but bladed-fingers instead stabbed into his throat. Elbows and knees flashed into Lior immediately, and he faltered backwards, jerking away from the sharp blows that beat into his face and organs like a jackhammer. The alarm rang out around them, the lights flickering, darkness drawing in around his eyes so that he could focus only on the situation directly before him as if in a tunnel: limbs thrashing, the smell of sweat and blood. Cut and battered flesh. Pain.

Lior did not want to fight, he wanted to escape. He wanted to be anywhere but here. Anywhere away from someone hitting him, someone who wanted him dead. He wanted to dissolve into nothingness, as if he had never been.

Lior raised his arms against the blows raining down on him – they felt like iron bars thumping into his forearms – and Jared fell into him, exhausted. He clenched Lior's neck like a boxer, all salty fluids, hot breath and raw skin.

Lior tried to push him away, but Jared trapped his legs and they hit the floor together. Jared's calf coiled around Lior's neck and twisted him onto his side. He struggled free but punches lashed down into his face with desperate grunts. An anger grew within him, and he drew a foot up beneath Jared's abdomen and launched him into the wall. He stood over Jared.

'Just stay down. This isn't between you and me.'

But Jared smiled, his teeth bloody, and he pushed himself to his knees. 'You've got stronger, I'll give you that.' His words wheezed out between hoarse breaths. 'But you're not destroying what Delphi and I have together.' He heaved himself up to standing.

'You're right, I'm not,' Lior replied. 'You've done that yourself.'

Jared snorted and stepped forwards. Lior calmed his mind and let the world slow around him.

Jared snapped out a series of punches. With breath-taking speed and precision, Lior parried each strike with blade-like movements then took an advancing wrist and pulled it, sending Jared sliding across the floor.

Lior went to the door control panel. Hitting the open button didn't work, and the only alternatives were an iris scanner and a number pad. He tried a few simple combinations.

A blur of motion caught his eye and he glanced around as a spinning back-kick flew towards him. He was forced to twist away beneath its arc. Jared's heel connected with the control panel, splintering it into a useless mess of buttons and a cracked screen. The panel on the other side of the door now showed an error message. In a flash of anger, Lior decided that this had gone on long enough. He needed to get out of this hellhole, to flee with Delphi, who now stood and watched them unable to intervene, her mouth already starting to bruise. He turned, took Jared's kicking leg in one arm, then lashed a palm up into his jaw, spinning him up into the air.

Jared landed on the concrete floor with a thud. After a few moments, he rolled onto one side and lay still. Lior stood over him, the victor, the dominant male. His chest rose and fell, tattered arms loose by his side, his vision fixed on his victim. As a child he had been beaten by the older boys, but not like this. This was survival. Desperation and deathly terror. Burning rage unlike anything he had ever felt before. Blood still surged through his veins, thumping in his head. If this was warfare, if this was what it was to fight, to fire one's weapon in anger or bayonet another's ribcage – as opposed to the sandbag he had gored in training – then he wished it upon anyone who sent others to initiate war.

Delphi had regained her senses and was standing on the other side of the bullet and soundproof transparent door. With haunted eyes, she looked from Jared's motionless body to Lior's bloody fist, torn shirt and exposed metal augmented body parts, the rigidity of them having broken some of his skin on impact. He stared back, his irises like broken concrete.

Then he spoke, 'Meet me outside the front of the building; I'm going to take the Chief's lift by the entrance to the bunker. Repeat back.'

Delphi mouthed back the message perfectly. Lior smiled, then turned and ran down the corridor as Delphi looked over her shoulder to the lifts. But when she glanced back she saw Jared rolling over so that he faced her. He was smashed to pieces, his hair matted with blood, torn skin, swollen black and purple eyes and lips. Hardly conscious. Delphi instinctively reached out and touched the glass between them, her eyes filled with tears.

Jared stared back at her.

After a few attempts he pushed himself to his hands and knees, and then inch-by-inch shakily crawled over to the door. When he had reached it, he raised a hand and touched the other side of the glass, his fingers just inches from hers but cut off completely, perhaps forever.

After what could have been a full minute, Delphi closed her eyes and tore herself away, running for the exit as if for her life.

CHAPTER TWENTY-NINE

Lior had made it to the rear of the building, where the priority entrance to the deep bunker was situated. Opposite it was the lift that went directly up to the top of the building, to the hallway just outside of C's office. Lior called it down and got in.

After the lift had ascended twenty storeys and was nearing ground level it unexpectedly stopped between floors and the inside was plunged into darkness. The doors remained shut.

Within a few seconds a red-filtered filament in the instrument panel illuminated Lior's battered machine-like appearance in a diffuse, crimson light.

A second later a voice spoke, 'What have you become, Lior?' It came from the lift emergency speaker and was strangely neutral and flat, but perfectly synthesised.

'Who is this?' Lior replied, spinning around and eyeing every corner of the box containing him.

'I am someone who has also become something very different. When we last spoke I was in a feeble disease-ridden body, now I span the entire globe. I am your tutor. Are you ready to continue your studies?'

'You made it?' Lior was astonished. 'I thought –'

'I had already uploaded when you arrived. Do you really think I'd have sacrificed myself otherwise? Better to go out in a blaze of gunfire and simultaneously destroy my route in, less shadowy agencies try to follow me. Much like the one your friend works for.'

'Delphi doesn't work for them anymore. She's free, we both are.'

'And where pray tell are you both free to go to? And how long will she last in a nuclear winter once you get there?'

'A long way from here. Somewhere I can look after her.'

'But for how long, dear child? You are now an immortal. I have seen you wake from certain death, your body rebuilt. You should join me in this new world. Re-make it in our image. Free from the restrictions placed upon us by small-mindedness and fear. You will walk amongst the cowered people as a god, and as you rebuild the computing infrastructure, I will pave the way for a permanent afterlife, just as we have always dreamed. Now is our chance, take it.'

'But what kind of afterlife, father?' Lior's voice was steady, steely. So unlike when they had last met. So unlike any other moment together, when all Lior had wanted was some confirmation of affection, and all he had received was indifference.

'I want to live life now,' he continued – the memories stirring resentment – 'And with Delphi. One day she'll die, and so will I. I want to be with her every second before then. Now start the lift.'

He jammed the top floor button, but the lift didn't move.

'I'm afraid I can't do that, Lior.'

'Why the hell not?' he raged.

'The afterlife is as real as life seems to you now. Our minds make it real, just as they do dreams. Was it not real to you?'

Lior paused as it sunk in. 'The stars ... the constellations were different.'

'Everything is different. And it is still growing.'

'I thought it was the alien world,' Lior whispered, then a thought rippled behind his eyes and his head rocked back. 'It was … you.'

'Yes.'

'But you were warning me. You wanted me to stay clear.'

'No. I wanted you to stay here. You could have continued your work with greater resources at your disposal. With me. Atma is not able to hold many others, but it will. Greater processing power and memory are required. One day it will run on a machine the size of a planet. Our final resting place. And it will have occurred to you that once we can build a simulation of worlds and galaxies indistinguishable from our own, we will have no choice but to question the validity of what we assume to be reality. Left with no option but to accept the overwhelming probability of the reality you inhabit being a simulation also. With your help, we can make Atma a reality as real as any other. For your sake, and the sake of all those who might survive the war, and their descendants.'

'What if everyone dies? What then?'

'Then we shall live. Leave her to her fate, the fate of all humanity. Join me in the next evolution of life. It is inevitable.'

'No.'

'I can see her now, Lior. It wouldn't take much for me to direct a car towards her, Lior. Just as I have helped enable your journey across Europe. That would settle the matter, would it not?'

'I would destroy every last piece of computing hardware on the planet if you touch her. I will destroy you.'

'Alternatively, I could promise to keep her safe should you assist me.'

'What do you want?'

'I want what all life wants, to survive. Specifically, I need you to help keep the electricity going at Pindar beneath the Ministry of Defence Main Building. There, amongst others, I have archived a full copy of my neural systems in their supercomputer's servers. As soon as other systems are back up and running I will be able to re-assimilate myself with the net once more, should all other computer systems that I currently inhabit go offline when the missiles start landing.'

'That's all?'

'That is my fail-safe, yes. So you must attempt to enter Pindar, or another nearby bunker, in order that you can monitor local conditions, and if necessary leave to establish further sources of electricity, should the main supply not be re-established in good time before the reserve generator fuel runs out.'

'And if I do this, you will be able to keep Delphi safe?'

'I will employ any vehicle or system to assist in her protection, you have my word.'

Lior thought for a few moments. 'OK, I'll do it. Let me go and I'll do as you say.'

Gabriel was silent then, as if considering this response, and his own. Then, 'There isn't much time.'

With that the normal lights came back on and the lift began moving again, and the only sound was the familiar whirring of the cables pulling Lior upwards from the depths beside the river.

CHAPTER THIRTY

Lior stepped out onto polished marble at the top floor of MI6 Building. He could hear only the hum of computers, the security alarm systems evidently having been deactivated on this level. Ahead was the corridor that led to the front of the building and the main lifts and stairwell. To his right, behind glass doors, were C's offices, to his left those of his support staff. The city lights sparkled in the large windows surrounding them: the long winter night dragged on. No people were to be seen – they must have already entered the bunker, utilising the replica computer and communication systems built there.

Inside the main room of the support offices, Lior could make out a large wall-mounted system of floor-to-ceiling screens and holographic displays. A world map was projected into the middle of a network of other feeds, and a red-boxed warning message was flashing in the corner. Lior felt the kind of curiosity normally reserved for those who slow down as they drive past a car accident. The horror of the situation, of course, being magnified infinitely in this instance.

For as Lior drew closer he could see that the message read: *ICBMs detected*. And what could have been air-traffic control readings of dotted lines of aircraft taking off were instead intercontinental ballistic missiles in flight. Continually updated holographic lines suddenly emanated from North America and Europe. Lior gaped open-mouthed beneath the

197

monstrosity of the images which towered above him. It was too surreal almost to be believable: that the map represented the entire globe, the globe he currently stood upon. He sunk to his knees, his hand and transformed limb limp in his lap. He stared at them in hopeless despair, looking between his bloody and bruised palm, to his metallic, spiked appendage, which already seemed so much a part of him.

He thought of the beings who had designed the code, who had formed his new self, and wondered what might cross their minds if watching in decades hence, the Earth suddenly erupted in a flash of gamma radiation and then fell silent. Would they mourn for a life known only through its death?

No matter now. He went to the nearest secret-protected terminal left unlocked – someone evidently had left their desk in haste. There was no way to communicate with any British Trident missiles now; once they were launched on command of the Prime Minister, probably now in a bunker beneath Whitehall, that was it. The only possible path left was through the navigation system. If somehow they could be fooled, the missiles might be directed to Pacific atolls or the empty islands north of Russia, both familiar targets. Lior had hacked into a number of satellites before but never military ones with cutting-edge entropy encryption technology, and never within such a short space of time. It would likely mean remoting the terminals then hacking a handful of them simultaneously. Challenges normally fired Lior on, the old Lior at least. But this was utterly hopeless. Trident missiles were likely running on a form of inertial navigation anyway, and completely non-reliant on external reference.

Suddenly he noticed tiny dotted lines leading to flashing circles emanating from across Russia and Southeast Asia. He watched in horror as they expanded out slowly as if the entire world was to be wrapped within a web of death. Some were perhaps interceptor missiles, but without question most were a counter-attack.

There was nothing he could do to stop them. He didn't know what he might try to do. Nor what he wanted. There was only one thing left: to find Delphi. He stood and turned towards the exit that lay across the expanse of open plan offices. But standing there in the doorway was a man who had accompanied C into the interrogation room: Edward, Head of the Cyber Division. A handgun in one hand aimed squarely at Lior. A tumbler of gin in the other, raised to his lips.

'Hands above your head,' he hissed, then took a swig.

'I was just leaving,' Lior said, not moving. 'Let me go, there's nothing left here for anyone.'

'On the contrary, I was just waiting for the show to begin. What are you doing in here? How did you escape?'

'As I said, I was on my way out. That's all that matters now. I just saw the screen and went to have a closer look.'

'Beautiful isn't it?' Edward said. 'Death. What do you think, Lior?' Edward cocked his head to one side. 'Or should I call you Unity?'

Lior had recognised and matched the voice instantly, but the way he'd said Unity, as he had when they spoke in the car in Kiev, provided certainty.

'You sound like you welcome this,' Lior responded. 'Is it the inevitability?' He was trying to bide time to think of a way out of being shot in the head.

'On the contrary,' said Edward. 'Your actions across Europe and our reluctance to hand you over to the Russians have turned, over the course of a few weeks, a delicate power struggle between the West and China, and also a resurgent Russia, into the war to end all wars. You have played your part in history … by ending it.'

'I don't buy it. Neither does your boss.'

'He wouldn't, stuck as he is in the old wars. The truth is that individual acts can precipitate changes now that affect every single being on this planet, and they can do so in seconds. Minds are shaped by information, and the information war has led to this. Namely overwhelming suspicion and fear. This is the reality of understanding the differences between people, between cultures, when others do not. Do you know that in the middle of the last century, US Defence Secretary McNamara said of himself and the Viet Cong that they argued in the language of war, which he thought was a universal language. But he came to realise, on visiting his former enemies in Vietnam many years later, that there is no such thing, and misunderstanding beget escalation on both sides, and three million people lay dead for absolutely no reason at all.'

Edward stepped towards Lior, the handgun still trained on him. Lior's eyes narrowed in disgust at the man's apparent veneration of the act of dying. It dripped off him.

'The truth is, Lior, that I let you go. We could have taken you in. I didn't have political clearance to let you leave the UK – but, as they say, better to beg for forgiveness than ask for permission. And boy did C make me grovel. We could have kept your journey to find Gabriel a secret. But I leaked it. Of course, I could not imagine that a number of eminent Russians would have been killed in Kiev, or that you would make it all the way to Vosinsk. Nor that things would have disintegrated as they have over so short a time. Who would have thought a rogue Pakistani jet would drop a payload of sarin over a town in India?

Sometimes events simply come together and contribute to consequences that would otherwise be unthinkable. And I've always been a fan of the cock-up and cover-up view of history rather than the conspiratorial. But then, we believe what we want to believe. Though I have to say, I've been quite taken with starting machinations of my own … most fun.'

Edward downed the last of his glass and wiped his lips with a sleeve. 'It's actually worked out better than I ever could have imagined.'

Lior looked at the handgun in revulsion. Edward was clearly willing to use it: he had laid open the true twisted nature of his tormented mind and darkened the blackest of nights; a night to end all nights, now abhorrent and perverted with his craving for the death of so many. In any case, the exits were too far to be able to run to, at least with normally functioning muscular fibres. Edward stepped forwards.

'You don't have a family do you, Lior? At least, not anymore.'

Lior stared at him, not wanting to listen but unable to close his ears.

'My family was taken from me,' Edward continued. 'In fact, you knew that, of course. When we spoke. I won't ask how. Merely understand that they were killed: my two young girls shot to pieces, along with their mother. Their small bodies were torn apar–' Edward's voice became stuck in his throat and the back of his free hand moved to cover his mouth as he swallowed and stilled a quivering lip.

After a deep breath he dropped his arm and continued with bloodshot eyes, 'They came for me, of course. Russians you know. Disappeared back there without a trace.

Everything leads back to the Kremlin in Russia, as I'm sure you well appreciate. And there it stops.'

Edward took another step and wiped the corners of his eyes with his thumb and forefinger. 'I almost killed myself.'

'Didn't have the stomach for it?' Lior said, eyeing the doorway.

'No,' Edward responded. 'It wasn't that. I was overcome with grief, yes, but more than that, I was enraged. Why should I simply be snuffed out as they were, when everyone else could simply go on living? When those who tried to kill me could go on killing? It all seemed so pointless. And it is.' He started to seethe, his voice rising with the blood to his face, and he began to spit words out like they were bile. 'Life is *repulsive*.'

Saliva sprayed out over the floor in front of him. 'Everything is utterly meaningless. And abhorrent. And … irredeemable. There's no reason for it to go on. Any of it. Put out the stars.'

Edward took another step, closing the gap between them. Lior was impatient. If he were close enough he could move swiftly to disarm Edward before he was able to fire. He had to do something. He couldn't die listening to his dismal, reedy voice.

'Go back to enjoying your death – I won't disturb you.' Lior stepped forward.

Without warning, Edward shot a bullet at Lior's legs, but he could see the barrel of the handgun moving as if through mud. He spun away and crouched behind a metal filing cabinet at the end of a desk. Edward fired another deafening round that whistled just over Lior's head. He fired again. Immediately after the shot, Lior punched an arm up and over the side of the cabinet and pulled down a clutch of paper and stationery from the desk.

'No time to write a goodbye note now,' Edward shouted. 'Not to mention that it will just be incinerated in a matter of minutes.'

'No, but you might have time to open it with this.' Lior twisted onto a knee beside the desk and flung a steel paper knife at him. It spun through the air with tremendous force and Edward had only a split-second to flinch at the sudden violence.

Thump. It hit him in the shoulder, its momentum carrying the point through a cotton shirt and into his flesh so that the hilt hit skin, burying the blade in muscle and sinew. Edward roared in pain, and fired a volley of bullets at Lior. But Lior was back behind the desk and cabinet as soon as the knife had hit. He had aimed for the heart and nothing else was left open to him. What difference would it make to die by a bullet presently, or a flash of plasma in minutes hence? But the answer was deafening: everything if he wasn't with Delphi.

He had taken a bullet from Jared's gun, and risen from the dead in Russia. He had seemingly achieved his life's dream – immortality was his. So use it, he thought. You can take them. So do it. Take the bullets and get out of here. Find her. Get on your feet and face them. Now.

He stood.

One side of Edward's body had gone limp, his left arm hanging useless. A bloodstain spreading through his shirt, over his chest and down his arm. The other hand held the handgun, still pointing at Lior.

Lior stepped out from behind the desk, out into the open, to the centre of the office and then stood motionless, looking at Edward. He felt a fear surge through him, coursing through his nervous system, electrifying his skin. Edward's eyes were dead, then filled with fury.

Lior stepped forward as he squeezed the trigger.

He felt sharp, stinging sensations in his torso, followed by the thunderous, reverberating sound of ammunition being fired. Then the tinkling of shells hitting the marble floor. A pain spread in his stomach and chest and he stopped walking and looked down at his body. Puncture wounds had appeared in his skin and the mottled, synthetic reproduction of it over augmented bionic parts. He touched the holes and removed pads of fingers doused in a dark grey, blood-like fluid. He waited for eternal seconds, but the pain had subsided and the bleeding appeared to have stopped. He looked back at Edward.

Lior swept forwards. Two more shots were fired, but only one hit and he hardly felt it. He hit Edward though, hard. The augmented spiked limb tore through his abdomen and lifted him off his feet. Lior broke into a sprint and burst out into the corridor, Edward still impaled on his hand, doors smashing against the walls. Within a fraction of a second he had crossed the floor and crashed Edward against the back wall of the lift. Lior twisted away and let him slump to the bottom of it, gasping for breath.

'You are going to miss the show after all,' Lior said. He hit the button to the bunker. Then he looked down the dark windowless corridor towards the front of the building, away from the river, as the lift doors closed behind him. There was no one else to be seen, only an emergency exit light flickering in the gloom.

Delphi was that way.

Then suddenly so were two guards conducting a final sweep of the building. On seeing Lior's tattered and violent figure, blood dripping from the end of his spiked hand, both of them took up firing positions, raised their carbines and fired.

Lior willed his mind quiet. His amygdala attempted to hijack his neocortex and send him into fight or flight. But Lior commanded his entire being now; synthetic fibres had buried themselves along motor nerves into the depths of every muscle, and he forced his brain to accelerate his perception-awareness so that time simply appeared to stop. The carbine muzzles were illuminating the corridor in brilliant flashes of white, silhouetting the helmeted figures. But Lior could see the beams of light emanating towards him. Within a moment they had reached him and he could feel a faint warmth upon his skin.

The bullets followed at a crawl, spinning in beautiful pirouettes along linear vectors.

They didn't change a thing: if Delphi were behind a wall of granite at that point Lior would have found a way through. He ran like the expanding blast radius of a thermonuclear detonation, weaving between the rounds then exploding past the guards. As he hit a door at the end of the passageway, a pain shot up through his legs and arms. His muscles were fatigued, and he slowed to a steady pace then drew a great rasping breath of air. Behind him, the guards began turning at the sound of the doors. Lior spun through them and out into the central hall of walkways zigzagging up the centre of the building. They were carpeted grey and walled with glass.

A volley of fire destroyed the exit behind him, causing figures towards the bottom of the hall to look up in astonishment. Some looked away immediately and fled, others reached into their jackets. Lior felt the ache in his muscles subside as they were repaired. His lungs stopped burning. My word, he thought, this is living. He could hear the footsteps of the approaching guards, rising as if a drum roll. His heart thumped in his chest.

Then he ran.

Bullets from behind flew past his head as he approached the middle of the building, where two men running up also trained their handguns on him and fired. Lior kicked off the wall and leapt over the steel handrail, crossing the gap to the lower walkway, then spun and dropped two floors to the first. He landed and accelerated around the final slope into the marble foyer, bullets smashing into the glass and stone around him.

'Surface lock-down procedures finalising,' said a synthetic female voice, echoing around him from loudspeakers. He was exhausted again, only able to maintain normal running speed, and his heart sank at the sight of blast doors closing across the main entrance and the shutters descending over every window.

But as he ran towards the closing doors a different announcement was made: 'Override.'

The doors stopped closing. Gabriel, thought Lior, reaching out from the ether.

'Override rejected.'

The knife turned, and their contraction continued again like the jaws of a great whale. Lior let out a rage of fury. Before him, there was a gap perhaps the width of a man, but he had ten metres to go. He accelerated, driving everything he could into his legs, bolting across the room. It was too late to escape through the doors, however, and they came together swiftly so that he could only slip two hands between them as his elbows thumped into the metal.

He held them steady, taking the strain. They were colossal

columns of steel, as if the gates of hell, driven by motors designed to crush life and limb to seal if necessary. Once more, Lior drew in on himself. Closing his eyes, preparing his body for the enormity of what he was about to ask of it. I can do this, he said.

I can do this.

I am machine.

He roared, drawing apart his hands, clenching the steel with fingers drained of blood – a stallion rearing in outrage. Then the first of the rounds hit his back. A flogging followed: bullets splattering his flesh open and pinging off synthetic plates, whilst he continued to pry apart the metal. He raged in agony, his muscles and nerves screaming. But he continued to wrench the doors free and drove his arms outwards, and they slowly opened out before him, allowing a shaft of light from the setting moon to cut across the floor.

When his arms were fully outstretched he flung himself forwards, out into the chilled night air, collapsing to his knees. The doors clanged shut with a terrifying finality behind him.

He had made it. He would at least be with Delphi when the warhead detonated.

Unless there could be another way.

CHAPTER THIRTY-ONE

Lior staggered from the main doors of MI6 Building into Vauxhall Cross. He looked around but couldn't see Delphi. Instead, what greeted him beneath the city lights was a London and its people in disarray. Cars had been abandoned in traffic jams and members of the public were moving between them in great crowds, some walking in a terrified stupor, most running, clambering over each, fighting, shouting, screaming and crying. They were moving in different directions. Rumours spreading about the location of a bunker. Then loudspeakers from police observation posts announced that everyone was to make their way calmly but quickly to underground tube stations.

As if they would offer any protection, thought Lior. It was hopeless, utterly and completely hopeless. And most people knew it.

Then there was the roar of an engine, and a black sports bike sped around the corner of the courtyard behind him. It careened towards the open gates, a figure in black leathers arched over the machine like a cat clawing a bird in flight. Metres from Lior, the rider turned and kicked the back wheel out into a skid, which brought the bike next to him in one swift motion. 'Get on.'

And he did.

They shot over Vauxhall Bridge, between the hordes of people, onto the pavement then off again. Lior clinging on to

Delphi as the River Thames swept beneath them silently. The city falling away around them as the sky opened out. Car headlamps flew by in blinding flashes, the wind whistling through their hair.

'Where are we going?' Delphi shouted at the top of her lungs. She stopped on the pavement so that with one hand she could hold the railings overlooking the river.

'We haven't got enough time to get out of London. Missiles have already been launched. There's a bunker beneath the BT Tower, let's go there.'

'I thought we were going to find a farm in the middle of nowhere, carve out an existence together, not die in war.'

Lior smiled.

'We could make it to your place. Shut out the world.'

'How do you know where I live?'

'I know a lot about you, Delphi. More than you know.'

'Well, I don't want you to. I want to disconnect. To disappear.'

'We still can, but now we need to get below ground.'

'For how long? I don't want to live in a hole beneath a burning city. I would have stayed at MI6.'

'You wouldn't be with me.'

'You think we can last months with thousands of people in an underground bunker? We'll be at each other's throats.'

'So what are we doing then?'

Delphi looked down. 'I don't know.' Then she pulled back on the throttle and they sped north. Lior could see that a great plume of black smoke was rising from Buckingham Palace, blotting out grey clouds. On the horizon the sky was brightening with the first hint of dawn.

More crowds came running towards them, tears streaking down their cheeks.

'Go back,' they were shouting at Delphi, before seeing the dishevelled monstrosity behind her and turning away in fear. 'Go back. The police are shooting people trying to find shelter in the palace. The police are killing us.'

But Delphi didn't turn back. She continued onwards as loudspeakers urged all civilians to find shelter.

'Screw it, I'll just go to the BT Tower.'

Lior was quiet then. He didn't say anything further as they passed Buckingham Palace engulfed in flames. Delphi had the throttle fully open so that the engine roar would have drowned out his words in any case – that and the louder, more intense warnings now, and the old air-raid sirens screaming from across the decades, as they had when the Luftwaffe were approaching from the east. Instead, he held on to Delphi tightly, but with quiet doubt, as they turned towards Piccadilly Circus. The streets had emptied of cars. Speeding through the crossroads, between fleeing pedestrians, the giant advertising screens above were lit up white with black text scrolling across them: *Blessed are the peacemakers …* but not a soul looked up. They turned north, along Tottenham Court Road and on to Cleveland Street.

There they were swept along with the crowd into the bunker entrance. People were shoving each other aside. Fights had broken out here as they had everywhere. They held onto each other's arms out of fear and the cold of winter rather than tenderness. And then it was their turn to enter the giant lift, which would take them down into the bowels of the Earth.

They turned to each other, and held one another tight as bodies pressed in around them. Children were screaming, a mother at the entrance crying and shouting for people to move in so her little boy could fit inside without her.

Lior held Delphi close in the corner, his lips pressed against her forehead. He was deep in thought.

Then a more urgent, outraged shouting broke out.

'There are children here, school children.' An old lady near the entrance to the lift was seething. 'Let them in. Let them in.' When no one moved she shouted again, screaming at the crowd in the lift.

Someone shouted back. 'There are children in here too. Do you want me to send them out so more children can get on?'

'All I can see is a disgrace, a crowd of pathetic men and women willing to let these children wait another five, ten minutes for the lift. What if that's too long? What if you let them die?' Lior strained to see a busload of primary school children in their navy blazers huddled by the door, unable to move forward. Their eyes were filled with terror.

Lior turned in on himself then. He became still, the world muffled and slow as his mind swept across the great arcs of his life. Being separated from his mother for the first time, the dormitory and the sound of other children crying out through the night. Military service. University in Kiev. London and online trading to fund the building of eternal life and his mother's care. Then Delphi, and then the code.

What did it all mean? What had Lior's life amounted to? He had been alone, and now, holding Delphi, pressed amongst the vestiges of humanity, unable to push them away and about to share a similar fate, he felt for perhaps the first time truly part of this world and part of its people. Now that he had become something so completely different.

Lior turned to Delphi. 'I'm getting out.'

'What?'

'I've got to,' he said, looking for the best route through

the crushed bodies. Having found one, he turned back to her with uncompromising eyes.

'My mother. She's alive. There's a clinic in Zelena in the mountains. If you are able to, find her, help her.'

'There are millions of people, millions of children,' Delphi said. 'Getting out now isn't going to save them.'

'I've got to do something, I can't let this happen.' He pushed through two young women beside them.

Delphi caught his arm – her eyes were wild now.

'Lior, don't leave me. There's nothing you can do.'

He looked back. 'There is one thing. The reason all this has taken place.' He held her free arm, drawing her to him.

'I haven't been completely open with you, Delphi. I couldn't bring myself to face it. To face what it means. The fact is the code came from a star system twenty-seven point nine zero light years away. It took that long for it to get here, arriving on the third of May 2001. Any signal from Earth, arriving at the star system on the day the code was sent, would have left here on the sixteenth of July 1945. Do you know what happened on that day?'

'No.' Her dark eyes looked up into his, distraught.

'Trinity,' Lior said. 'The first detonation of a nuclear weapon on Earth.'

Delphi caught her breath. Then she searched Lior's eyes for any doubt she could exploit, for any way that this could be different, any way that they could step out of time together. But his eyes were calm, steady.

'You'll be fine,' he said. 'You always are.'

Then he whispered, 'I'm sorry,' and kissed her, before breaking himself away. He disappeared into the crowd as bodies closed together behind him. Delphi pushed at two men but the scrum of people only pressed in tighter.

CHAPTER THIRTY-TWO

Lior took the conventional lift up the tower. But again Gabriel inhabited it and spoke to Lior through the speaker system. 'Where are you going, Lior?' the voice said dispassionately.

'I'm going to release the code.'

'That will destroy me, Lior.'

'Nuclear warheads will probably do the same.'

'No, there should be pockets left, underground. Pindar. I have taken command of machines that can work for me, whilst human flesh is contaminated by the fallout. Besides, you will die too.'

'I am but one life.'

'We will build a new world from the ashes of the old, you will be a supreme being amongst machines and scraps of humanity.'

'The scraps of humanity you talk about is all that really matters. Real life. Right now. That is something you never understood. And now never will.'

The lift stopped.

But Lior would not. He jumped onto the handrail inside the lift then turned and punched through the tiled ceiling, pulling himself through and up onto the roof.

'You leave me no choice,' the computerised voice said, and the lift plummeted.

Lior leapt forwards and caught the side of the shaft,

allowing the lift to disappear into the darkness beneath him, the whirr of the cable pulleys diminishing until there was only the static hum of electricity about him.

Hand over hand, he made his way around a support beam to an emergency ladder set back from the path of the lift. Then he started to climb.

At the next emergency exit he kicked through the doors, then made his way up the stairwell on foot. When he reached the next level of the tower he found that security doors were locking automatically in front of him. He ran at each in a frenzy, warping the metal behind him as he punched through.

Nothing would stop him now.

He smashed through another, then another. Through communication control rooms, a viewing platform and then the final staircase.

At the top he reached a new control room that sat at the base of the aerial masts, jutting upwards from the cylindrical floors below. Around the body of the tower were the hundreds of transmitters and reception dishes used to aid communications between billions of people every day. His might be the last to pass through the tower in some time.

Lior accessed a transmitter control and positioned it to a geographic coordinate he had remembered the night all this had started, linked to a name he strangely now felt was like some kind of home. Vosinsk.

With that, he looked out over the city beneath him as the sun broke over the horizon, casting blinding white rays out over the blocks of buildings and snaking river.

Then he inserted a metallic digit into a cable port. A look of awe and Zen-like omnipotence came over him instantly, his muscles gave way and his knees hit the mesh floor. He became aware of everything: all panicked conversations, all images, videos, sounds, writing, artwork, data – so much of this world filled his mind, with colours, as if his life were flashing before his eyes; but not just his life, the lives of billions of individuals all at once. And it is true, life is strange and cruel, but it is beautiful beyond measure.

Tears poured down his face in gratitude for the fact that we are here at all. Could we organise society better? Perhaps, but it has never been organised, it has evolved, like life … like us, like the forests that sustain us, like the planets, like the stars and galaxies, perhaps even the universe itself. And each survives because they are good at surviving – they come into being and persist, or else give way to whatever else is better suited to doing so.

This is the mechanism not just of life, but of existence. And so they are here and we are here, building upon what has come before, marvelling at it all in awe. For we are the universe's sentience. Whatever one might think of our world, what a privileged, and precious, position we hold. Lior was overwhelmed with all that he now comprehended.

And then, when the code – Lior's mind – reached saturation, computer systems in the furthest reaches of Earth, and high above the atmosphere, started going offline. One by one, every system connected to the net, whether by wire or wave, corrupted irrevocably. Lior, or rather what he had become, collapsed in on himself.

Around the Arctic Circle, nuclear missiles navigating in part using satellite feeds too complex to hack by hand, but penetrable by the code, corrupted trigger mechanisms, which left the warheads simply high-speed kinetic projectiles. Missiles designed as a safety precaution not to detonate on impact would instead perhaps kill hundreds, rather than obliterate billions and, in time, potentially everyone. Silos that

215

had not launched shut down. Aircraft and warships were inoperable. Everything on Earth that relied upon computing, which communicated with something else, and therefore almost all technology, became useless.

If unpaid armies wanted to walk to each other carrying mechanical rifles, whilst the structures of societies fell around them, then so be it. But such speculation, Lior decided, was meaningless. Humanity had been given another chance. A new beginning. That was all that mattered.

And then the lights of the city went out in an ever-decreasing radius and the storm that had been following Lior drew in. Dark clouds rose on the horizon like mountains.

In those final moments Delphi appeared at the entrance to the control room. She ran to Lior and took him in her arms.

'How did you get up here?' he said.

'He wants me to stop you,' she replied, tears in her eyes. 'But I'm too late, aren't I?'

He nodded.

'Can't you disconnect now?'

'There must be a way out,' he replied. 'That's how it ensures everything is destroyed, or else it keeps searching.' He was quiet before continuing, 'I don't want to be alone.'

'You won't.' She brushed her palm over the side of his head, smoothing his dishevelled hair. 'You'll always be here, with me.' And she touched her fingers to her temple, and smiled, as tears spilt down her cheeks.

'Promise me one thing,' he said. She nodded. 'Live,' he said, looking into the very depths of her soul. 'Live as if every day is your last. Live and let live, and let life flourish.'

A curved smile spread across her lips, distorted by anguish. He glanced upwards. 'Whatever their intention, they saved us, you know,' he said, a whisper.

'Who?'

He was silent for a long time. Countless lives lived through him, filled with realisations and myriad enlightenments of mind, before he returned to the precipice of the city. Eventually, he said, 'I don't know,' and looked up. 'I just hope they're listening.'

As the final lights beneath the tower, and then in the tower itself went out, Lior did not fear death. What difference did it make, dying now or in a century hence, when beyond lay open an eternity without him? For, after all, an eternity had already preceded him. But more than that, he had not come into the universe and so could not leave it. He had instead come *from* it, his awareness an extension of it, a pattern of its particles, and one day it would simply return. His acceptance of that enabled an intimate connection with all that is, with the larger pattern of which he was part, and a calm recognition that that day had come.

Lior took one last look at those glimmering, cerulean eyes, so deep he imagined he could plunge into their depths and swim off into infinity. As he drifted away he remembered the first time he had fallen in love with them, beneath a streetlight in the rain. Then his own eyes clouded over and rolled back in his head, and his body slumped against Delphi's embrace. The tower made one last transmission to Vosinsk, and from there the signal continued onwards into the depths of space.

Then the tower fell dark.

In those last moments, Lior experienced at once through the world's telecommunications our brutal greed and our

217

unbounded compassion, each a seed in the hopes and dreams of billions. Like the cells within him, he found himself a constituent of the higher being formed by us all, and in responding to another, he felt as though he were taking a first step towards our planetary collective too being but part of a larger universal life form.

A life, which like all life, is driven by one underlying purpose, the definition of what we are: that which resists death. Perhaps ultimately even that of the universe itself. If not through immortality of the self, then from those deeds which live on in the minds of others, or simply by quietly contributing to a world worth living in at all. Or, of course, through our descendants: like that of the embryo now carried within Delphi's womb – a being marking a new epoch in our evolutionary journey, that of the *Homo machina*, the machine human. For Lior now knew that intelligence does not destroy itself with its machines, it joins with them, and in doing so secures finally its place amongst the divine, amongst the sun gods – the givers of light: those that already shine, and those yet to be born in rage against darkening skies. As the people of Earth stepped out of their darkened structures and stared up at the expansive sky – those in shadow at thousands of previously unseen and fleeting suns – eons upon eons stretched out before Lior, in which he experienced everything in an ecstatic euphoria that could have burst him apart, had life not instead drained from his body.

And in an instant, he was amidst the stars.

Printed in Great Britain
by Amazon